The Origin of Tormenta Cubano

GUILLERMO F. PORRO III

The Origin of Tormenta Cubano

For information about this title or to order other books and/or electronic media, contact:
Guillermo Porro
dadeshark19@yahoo.com

ISBN: 978-1-087-84163-2 Paperback

Printed in the United States of America
Cover and Interior Design: Infinity Flower Publishing, LLC

In dedication to Lord Collins Sita and Austin G. Baucom a.k.a the original Loca Manzana for providing me with motivation and inspiration to right such a fun mix of English and Spanish.

CHAPTER 1

When you think about Cuba you think culture, passion, baseball, and palm trees amongst other things. However, one thing you do not include with the Cuban history is the heroes in armor or genetically gifted. Well, it is because you are not in the right section of your library, or you are not listening to the streets. You see, between the palm fronds and the Caribbean sun, Cuba struggles to keep itself apart from an ever-changing world. Even as the flavors and smells change through the decades, the heart of Cuba remains strong and powerful - just like the core of all people on the island which contains their passion and culture - plus a dose of Cafecito.

Cutting and twisting our way through the streets toward the plaza, his legend brings back stories like the ones of heroes that remain miles away. From armor to mutations, heroes like these do not venture into the Cuban timeline except for once during a time when Cuba stood in the crosshairs. His name is not spoken in any book but is passed on by generations as they share stories and pass an occasional black and white picture. He is Tormenta Cubano, and he was the one who brought forth justice during a time of unsettlement. The time was October 1962 and tensions between countries were at an all-time high. Then one day like a storm surge coming off the ocean, Tormenta Cubano came forth with an array of powers only seen in foreign war zones.

Now one man can only properly tell his origin and the stories of his heroism. The man who lived and overcame the odds of every gang or military he ever came up against. However, as the years pass, the warfare has taken a toll on his body and mind that things have been forgotten. So, I Mario his best friend and sidekick must keep his origin alive so future generations can know his truth. Let me introduce you to the story of the Tormenta Cubano.

Spinning our attention from the Plaza Vieja toward a nearby park, you can see the aging facade along with the clanging of baseballs flying from the field. Now beyond the men in their tattered uniforms hitting ground balls sits a single man at a park bench. With his back up against it, he shows off his tan skin and the scars that lace throughout. Wearing a white Guayabera and long trousers, the man tries to hide himself in the shade of the palm trees. His hat sneaking below his black eyebrows, he watches as a pair of old Chevrolet Impalas drive past when his attention shifts back with the crack of the bat. Hiding in his shirt pocket, a single cigar sits inside even as the man watches as one of the gentleman trots around one of the bases.

"Buen lugar para ver el juego," a voice says, placing a smile on the man's face. He then shakes his head before turning his attention to the left where he sees a young man similar in looks to his own making his way closer.

"Han mejorado desde el año pasado," the man replies as he watches the young man sit beside him on the bench. Getting comfortable yet keeping his distance, the two men place their elbows on their thighs while resting their hands over their dark facial hairs.

"Al menos se quedaron en casa en lugar de ir más allá del oleaje," the younger man says as he sits back on the bench.

"Ellos son los afortunados," the older man replies, turning to the younger man as the bat in the field cracks as it makes contact. Before the man can reply, they both turn to watch as the ball flies past the infield and over the field of brownish grass. Heading toward the leaning wall around the outfield, the ball falls feet shy as the sound of men cheering takes hold of the space. Turning their attention back to the men, they watch as the batter jogs around the bases as the others nod and applaud.

"Papa, no quise decirlo de esa forma," the younger man replies as they continue to watch the next man approach the plate with the bat in hand. Silently, they observe as the man prepares himself by striking the bat against his shins before placing it atop his shoulder. Then with a wind up, the pitcher unleashes the ball toward him as he swings it upon its approach. Once again, the ball connects with the bat except it ricochets through the shreds of rusty cage. Zipping through the air, the ball aims at the younger man as he struggles to make a move.

"Diego, Quitate del camino," the older man yells as he watches him struggle to move out of the way. Realizing he was not going to move in time, Diego's eyes shut as the man watches as he braces for impact. However, before the ball comes close, the older man extends out his hand as the ball collides with his palm allowing him to wrap his fingers around it. Feeling nothing, Diego opens his eyes to see the back of his dad's hand in front of him before he pulls it back.

Turning his attention to his dad's face, he sees an emotionless gaze as he brings his hand closer as Diego struggles to bounce between his dad and the men in the field.

"Estas bien?" the men yell from the field. Turning toward his dad, he watches as he clenches his fist and stands up from the bench. Erasing every inch of the ball within his grasp, his dad looks up with a fiery rage as the muscles in his arm strain and flex. Then with a single crunch, they watch as a beige powder slips from between his fingers toward the sandy soil. After taking a couple of steps, Diego watches as his dad turns toward him before turning to the men with their hands up against the cage.

"No te preocupes por eso," his dad says before shifting toward his attention to the Plaza and the fountain sitting in the center. Walking faster, he crosses the street after watching the Metrobus pull away from the curb. Once he was safe across the street, Diego turns toward the scowling group before looking down at the powder sitting in a pile along the dirt. Shrugging his shoulders, he grimaces as he looks over to his dad, not giving a second thought to any of the group.

"Ven aqui," the men yell as Diego darts over toward the street as four cars pass him by.

Watching as his dad remains aside the fountain, he waits for the street to clear before crossing as he tries to wave his hands back and forth. Unable to catch his attention, he starts to sprint over as his feet land atop the brick-like sidewalk lining the street. Avoiding the cracks for superstition, he slows to a walk as he catches his dad with his hands atop the cement lining around the fountain.

Brick by brick, he makes his way closer as he watches his hands close against the cement as his face reddens. Steam starts to escape from his nose and lips as Diego approaches him before stopping just shy. Then just as his momentum comes to a stop, the sounds of thundering footsteps catch the attention of both Diego and his dad. They both turn back to see the baseball players with their bats hanging over their shoulders. Hats turn back, they gang up on them as they surround every escape. Huffing and puffing, they step closer as the other pedestrians start to run away.

"Nosotros no queremos problemas," Diego's dad says as he places a hand in front of Diego. Sending him back a step, he steps up as one of the men charges forward with bat in hand. Bringing down an attack with hopes of hitting a home run, the man slams the bat down only to catch nothing but air. They then watch as he grabs hold of the man's bat before ripping it from his possession. As his attention remains on the man, another of his friends' charges from the left side and attempts to tackle him down. As he extends his arms out, Diego's dad steps forward, and then slams the bat down into the man's back. Crumbling into the bricks below, he groans as the rest of the group takes a step back.

"Como te llamas Viejo?" one of the men asks as the rest of the group take another step back.

"Esteban Morales," Diego's dad replies before throwing the bat at the man who catches it after watching it bounce between his hands.

Their eyes widen as they stand frozen in front of the two as the hurt man limps toward the rest of the group. Once he is halfway there, two of them charge forward and grab him as they drag him toward the rest of the men. As their eyes widen, they whisper amongst themselves before watching Esteban approach the fountain. Continuing to look, he reaches down with a splash as the rest of the group try to see what is going on.

"Papa, ¿que estas haciendo?" Diego asks as he takes a step toward his dad. Without a reply, his dad looks back, picking his arm out from the water revealing the ball within his grasp. Diego looks on in surprise as his dad steps past him as he approaches the group of men.

"Sera major que traten esta pelota con respeto," Esteban says as he rolls the ball over to the men. Stopping with a bounce up against the front of his foot, the man picks it up with eyes as wide as the ocean.

While picking it up, Esteban watches as his sight switches toward the playing field as a bunch of players appear. Covering the bases and filling the rusty metal dugouts, crowds of shadows start to cheer as he can faintly hear the announcer. As time around slows, he hears the crack of the bat as he watches as the audience jeers as the ball flies back over the fence. Flying amongst the rows of trees, it lands just beyond the edge of the street before bouncing repeatedly atop the plaza. Bouncing past him, Esteban follows it until he watches as it lands with a touchdown in the fountain. As the water lifts just over top of the barrier, it sinks back as time returns to current events. Shaking his head, he turns toward the men as they gather around the man as he holds the ball in front of him.

"Como supiste que estaba ahi?" the man asks as he lobs it over to another who holds a bat up against his opposite shoulder.

"Vi al hombre golpearlo alli hace mucho tiempo," Esteban replies as Diego takes a couple of steps beside him. After a couple of seconds pass, their moods lighten as their scowls fade. Then with a nod, the men take off toward the playing field on the other side of the street.

Once they were gone, Diego turns to his dad as he looks back at him.

"Que fue eso?" Diego asks his dad as once more he turns toward the fountain as the waters hides behind a cloud floating above.

"No te preocupes hijo mio pero no le cuentes a mama lo que paso," Esteban replies as he once more leans over the edge of the fountain. Catching sight of his reflection in the still water, he looks over to his side to see Diego appear on the surface.

"Ademas quiero que mama prepare un almuerzo," Diego says as he turns to his dad who nods his head.

"Si, mi hijo, vamonos," Esteban replies as he dips his hands into the water before splashing his face. As the surface restores itself, he turns back to Diego who steps back before they both turn toward the sidewalk. Watching the cars as they pass, they catch sight of an old chevy making its approach. Extending out his hand, Diego steps past Esteban as they watch the car swerve over to them. Once its tires were even with the sidewalk, the car stops as the engine continues to rumble. Exhaust fumes spreading throughout the air, they approach the front of the red vehicle before ducking down to the opening in the door.

CHAPTER 2

As Diego pokes his head in, Esteban looks around at the surrounding plaza and the diverse mix of people walking throughout. After a few minutes, Diego stands up and looks over at Esteban before nodding with a smirk.

"Vamos Papa," Diego says as he opens the passenger door. Making his way toward the car, Esteban is first to settle on the uncomfortable cushions before Diego goes inside as well. With a slam of the door, the car takes off back into traffic as it makes the first right. Passing the plaza, the car enters the heart of the city as fading colors on the buildings start to blend. To their side, they watch as the people walking along the street travel up and down like a current.

"La tierra que el tiempo olvido," the driver says as both Esteban and Diego turn their heads straight.

"Es pero sigue siendo tan magnifico," Esteban says as he watches as the man's attention momentarily shifts toward him in the backseat. Looking away as soon as they make eye contact, the driver tightens his grip on the steering wheel as the chorus of sounds take over.

"Puedo hacerle una pregunta?" the driver asks when suddenly a horn blares out causing a moment of silence.

"Adelante," Esteban replies as he looks down at his hands and the scars that riddle over his skin. Beads of sweat slipping down his face, he looks upward to see the man's eyes looking into the rear-view mirror.

"Trabajaste en los campos de Caña de azucar?" the man asks, allowing Esteban to take a breath as the man turns his attention as he shifts lanes.

"Si, hace mucho tiempo," Esteban replies as he places his hands back down onto his lap. As the man nods his head, he looks up at the yellow light as he sneaks beneath it when suddenly a horn sounds as screeching intertwines with it. After a moment of screaming, their eyes shut as the inside of the vehicle jars around. Shifting its location a few feet, the two cars come to a stop along the side of the road as people start to gather around. Chattering about, smoke starts to grow as the smell of burnt rubber fills the surrounding area. The first to escape were the two drivers who stumbled out of their cars with bumps and bruises. Blood dripping down their faces, the driver of the taxi steps out with a groan as immediately he disappears into a plume of steam and smoke.

Meanwhile in the backseat, Diego's head droops down into his lap as Esteban turns over to him. Frantic at the sight of his son, he tries to nudge him back to consciousness as the sound of sirens starts to grow louder. After a couple of tries and a slight groan, Esteban starts to panic as he undoes both his and his son's seatbelts. Dangling between their bodies and the doors, Esteban looks over toward the window to see the other car blocking an escape. Before he can shift his attention, a series of knocks rings on the glass of the window. Turning, his eyes widen as he sees a face from his past.

"Colonel Lins," Esteban says as anger grows from the depths of his body. He watches as the tan face shift over as a bloody hand motion to someone out of view. Feeling unable to move, the face turns back to reveal the sight of another face, replacing that of Colonel Lins. Struggling to shake the image he had seen; Esteban shifts his focus when remembers his injured son beside him. Turning toward him as once more he groans, he catches sight of blood dripping down from his forehead onto his lap. Turning back, the person was gone as he presses his hands and face onto the smudgy window. Seeing no one close by beyond the gathering group of civilians, Esteban rubs his eyes before turning his attention to Diego.

"Papa," Diego groans, sending a chill down his spine as he starts to hear sirens echo through the open door. Before he can make a move, smoke starts to enter through the vents in the front which starts to cause him to panic. Gulping down his fear, Esteban turns to the window as flames build within his irises.

"Nosotros estamos saliendo de aqui," Esteban says as steam starts to pulse with every exhale. He then turns his attention fully on the door when he unloads a fireball which engulfs the entire frame. Erupting it from the hinges, the door lands on the ground before sliding to a stop just at the edge of the street. Behind it, the flame extinguishes as suddenly as it appeared, leaving nothing but a trail of smoke. Watching as the group ducks down, Esteban turns to Diego who struggles to keep himself upright. With no hesitation, he reaches over, and grabs hold of Diego before turning his attention to the opening to the outside. Quickly, he steps out into the open air with his son beside him. Just as they get their bearings, the ambulance pulls up with its sirens blaring.

Seeing it stop feet from the scene, Esteban looks around at the accident, realizing that both drivers are gone. Looking for a blood trail or an injured person, he finds nothing beyond the two cars that remain broken in the road. Before he could continue, the doors to the ambulance burst open as a pair of paramedics explode from out the back. One carrying a bag while the other charges forth, the two men catch Esteban's attention as he points toward his son. Upon their arrival, he hands off Diego to the two and allows them to sit him down along the ground. As they inspect his wounds, another pair of men push out the stretcher from the back and rapidly bring it over to where Diego is. As the first two lift him up, they bring him cautiously over to the stretcher as Esteban watches silently.

"A qué hospital lo llevaran también?" Esteban asks, causing the paramedics to shift their attention. Looking at him, the two closest to him step forward as the others push the stretcher back into the ambulance. Once Diego was safe inside, they shut the door, momentarily causing Esteban to shift his gaze back to the door before looking toward the two men.

"Eres pariente de ei?" one of the paramedics asked as the other took a step toward the ambulance.

"Soy su padre," Esteban says as he watches the other gentlemen stop in his tracks before looking over to the paramedic. The two come together as he whispers something into the others ear, maintaining eye contact with Esteban.

"Senor, esta Seguro de que esta bien?" the paramedic asks as the two start to examine Esteban from top to bottom.

"Estoy Bien, ahora dime a donde llevas a mi hijo," Esteban yells as the two men look at one another once more. The man on the right nods before turning his head in confusion. Hesitantly, they look again at one another when suddenly Esteban's anger takes hold as he takes a step forward which causes the street to shake and indent. As the shockwaves circle outwards, the group of people start to scream for a moment when it suddenly changes to laughter. Hearing the change, Esteban shifts his attention to the crowd when his eyes widen to his surprise when he sees face after face of the one from the window. Their brown eyes sitting within tan faces, Esteban watches as they start to laugh hysterically.

"Su padre murio en 1963," a voice says, causing Esteban to shift his attention only to find the two paramedics gone and two copies of the same being. They start to chuckle along with the crowd when one of them lifts a skeletal hand, dropping the sleeve of his military jacket. With a snap of his fingers, the ambulance starts its sirens which sends a reverberation through the surrounding area. Speeding through the road, it takes off as it begins to get farther away.

"Esto es imposible estas muerto," Esteban yells, attempting to charge forward only to watch the two step closer. Preventing him from going further on foot, Esteban turns his attention to the sky as he presses his feet into the asphalt caving it in further. Attempting to use the force to blast off, he extends his arms to no avail as the two men start to laugh once more. Looking back down, the two men are gone even as their chuckles remain. The road also remains clear, causing Esteban to turn his attention to the crowd to find no one standing there. Gone was the blood, broken glass, even the two cars and in their place was just the blank canvass of the empty road. Spinning around, watching as the world around him empties further, Esteban drops his head into his hands as the world continues to spin.

"DIEGO, DONDE ESTAS?" Esteban screams as he lets loose a blast of fire from the depths of his chest into the air.

Suddenly, the sun goes out along with every source of light absorbing the land in darkness when suddenly with a gasp, Esteban wakes up from the nightmare. Sweat pouring down his face, he throws off the linen sheet as he kicks his feet off the end of the bed. Placing his hands onto his face, he pulls his hands down, tearing off some of the sweat remnants. Keeping his eyes shut, his hands fall to his side as he reopens them to look at the door that stands feet away. Shaking his head, he walks forward, and grabs hold of the doorknob. Then with a single twist, he rips the hinges off the wall before tossing it into an open corner in the room behind him. Unable to care less, he keeps his head forward, revealing the faintly lit room that hid beyond the doorframe.

Stepping through, his eyes turn to the left to see a shelf of books when to the right he sees an old loveseat sitting in front of an old tv. Shooting out static, his blurry vision clears as he spots his wife sitting on the cushion as she smiles when their eyes make contact. Lorenza was the ounce of normalcy for Esteban as underneath her caramel exterior and her Latin features was a good soul and heart. Coming from the poverty of Havana, she has grown for an appreciation of the good people that exist beneath the cover of a land that time forgot.

"Otra Pesadilla?" Lorenza asks.

"Si, y esta vez vi una cara que no había visto en décadas," Esteban replies as he looks over at the bookshelf. As his eyes look it over, the surfaces flicker as he turns his attention to Lorenza. Seeing the same flicker as he shifts his sight toward her, the confusion erases itself when he sees her smile. Seeing her in all her beauty, initially he smiles as love takes over him only to have it change to confusion as her body starts to blur. The smile drops to a frown as he charges toward her only to be stopped by an invisible barrier. Crashing down to the ground, Esteban looks up in confusion as his cheeks and throat redden. As the flames build, section after section of the room start to come down, revealing the truth behind it.

Eyes as wide as plates, Esteban watches as more of the room reveals a more metallic interior. Silvers and whites from top to bottom, bars appear from thin air as the final streak of Lorenza's image fades away. Once the final spot is gone, Esteban's anger intensifies as beyond the barrier he spots several scientists in lab jackets making their way back and forth. Stopping in front of a board with flashing red lights, they push a couple before hitting a switch. Once the click echoes loudly, they turn toward the open doorway and start to make their way around.

"Dejame salir de aqui," Esteban roars as he approaches the bars. Intensifying his anger, the two men keep their attention on the open doorway as they grow closer. With slight smirks, they make their way into the darkness as the sounds of their footsteps fade away. As the silence consumes the room, Esteban steps back from the bars as the flames from within his chest shift toward his fist. Then with the might of his anger, he punches the surface as flames leech out from his skin. Making a connection, it dents the metal as he pulls his hand back before placing it to his side. Exhaling a bit of relief, smoke blows from his nostrils as he turns his back on the bars. Looking around the backside of the room seeing nothing but white walls, another set of footsteps triggers his hearing.

Turning his attention back, he watches as from out of the darkness, the two scientists return except this time behind them are a pair of guards. Spotting a briefcase in the hand of one of the men, the four line up just feet from the bars, admiring the indentation on the bar before smirking at Esteban.

"Impresionante que rompieras las dos capas de alucinacion," one of the scientists says as the rest of the group nods.

"Alucinaciones?" Esteban asks as his skin starts to radiate a reddish glow.

"Si," the other scientist replies as he points to the part of the room that he had not seen. Shifting his sight, he sees a metal bed frame and a plastic tray broken in half underneath it. Struggling to comprehend, he cautiously makes his way toward it as he kneels beside it. Tilting his head to the side, he picks up both sides as they crumble within his grasp.

"Que se supone que es esto?" Esteban asks as he turns his head even as he remains in front of the bed.

"Recuerdas ese puerta que tiraste con facilidad?" another voice asks, turning Esteban's attention back to the open doorway. Before his eyes, a man from his past steps out from the darkness. About six feet tall, the slender man comes into the light, wearing a lab coat as it hides the tropical button-down shirt underneath. His hair of salt and pepper mix remains still as he turns his attention to Esteban revealing his brown eyes. Grinning as he gets closer to the group, he watches as the man stops in the middle as the others split.

"TODOS SALUDEN AL COLONEL LINS," one of the guards say as

the rest of the men cheer as they drop to a kneel.

"Esto es imposible te vi estrellarte contra el aqua," Esteban says as he recognizes Col. Lins from his past. Searching his fuzzy memory for the time of his death, Esteban places his hands on his head as a headache causes his skull to tremble. Then suddenly he unlocks it as he starts to see a black car with the roof down swerving through the white lines in the road. Flames blazing the trail, the sight shifts as the man maniacally laughs out the window. Suddenly, the road curves around the cliff as the opening between sections of rusty metal guard rails grows larger. Revealing a pristine view of the Atlantic Ocean, his eyes widen in fear when he sees a herd of white tail deer sitting in the center of it. Munching on the grass that sits in the cracks between the broken chunks of asphalt, the deer look up as the car approaches. Before they can jump out of the way, the man screams as he attempts to swerve out of the way when he crashes into the back side of the last deer.

Struggling to regain control, the car starts to spin as it splits the rail before going over the cliff. Dropping with a scream the car falls toward the depths of the smooth blue surface. Landing with a thud, water geysers upward as it falls toward the ground. Then amid the scene, a shadow appears along the broken headlight and bumpers as they sit feet from the end of the road. Landing with a knee and fist to the ground, the sight shifts as Esteban makes his way toward the edge of the cliff. Seeing no trace of the car as it sinks further, Esteban turns toward the sporadic trees along the opposite side. Before he can see anything more than the escaping deer, the memory fades as he finds himself once more inside the cell before Col. Lins and his group of scientists.

"El Tormento Cubano penso que habia vencido al poderoso Col. Lins," Col. Lins says as the rest of the group start to chuckle.

Growing madder by the second, Esteban screams as he unleashes a flurry of punches, which dent the bars while sending chunks of plaster downward. Then before he can deliver another, he pauses when he watches Col. Lins snap his fingers. Shifting their attention, they listen as the sound of footsteps start to echo as a familiar wail slides between the steps

"Deja ir a la nino," Esteban yells, wrapping his hands around the bars of the cell.

"Entonces daños lo que queremos," the scientist replies as before another word can be spoken, a child appears from out of the darkness. Dragging behind another set of guards with guns, the kid attempts to drag his feet to slow the pace. Dirty and bloody, he tries to shake free up until the moment the guards arrive at the rest of the group. Realizing the stop, the kid shifts his attention around the room when he makes eye contact with Esteban. Returning a glimmer of hope in his eyes, the kid struggles to smile when the guards shove him to the ground. Groaning in pain, Esteban pounds the bars before shaking them violently.

"Que más quieres de mí?" Esteban screams as a pair of tears shrivel down his cheek. Pulling his hands back from the bars, he turns his arm over, so his palm faces upward. Revealing the track marks as they spread toward his wrist, Esteban scowls as he unrolls his sleeve to cover them back up.

"Lo suficiente para que mis hermaños y yo seamos imparables," Col. Lins replies as he turns to the scientist. Watching as he opens the briefcase, Esteban looks on as the scientist pulls out a syringe with a sharp needle at the end. Flicking a few drops of a clear liquid from out of the lumen, the scientist turns to Esteban as his scowl turns sour as his bottom lip quivers with rage.

Clenching his fist, the guards shove the kid forward causing him to scream which diffuses Esteban's rage momentarily. Watching as another guard walks off toward the control panel, he kneels in front of a storage unit and opens the lid. Watching as the steam rises out, the guard reaches inside when suddenly Col. Lins starts to cough repeatedly. Placing his hand up against his mouth, he turns toward the guard as he looks back up even as his hand remains in the unit.

"Consigueme mi dosis diaria idiota," Col. Lins yells as he places his hand down to his side. Resisiting the urge to cough some more, he watches as the man pulls out a single clear vial and a generic can from within the storage unit. Closing it, the guard shifts his attention back toward the group and makes his way. After another bout of coughing, Col. Lins watches as the man arrives before handing him the can before peeling the lid off the top. Taking a couple of swigs, the group sees the relief in Col. Lins's face as he exhales before turning his attention back to the rest of the group. Taking a first step, he pauses suddenly when he starts to hear Col. Lins swish back and forth, shifting everyone's attention.

"Que tipo es este?" Col. Lins asks as he looks down at the can. Watching as the mahogany brown liquid spins about with each movement of the can, Col. Lins frowns as he looks up at the man.

"Se llama cola Americana," the man replies to the displeasure of Col. Lins.

"Como se atreven esos cerdos Americaños a llamar a esto cola?" Col. Lins screams as he slams the can into the floor. As the remnants of the liquid spew from the container, it spreads onto the legs of the guards nearby. Trying to shake it off, the scientist's eyes widen as he attempts to avoid eye contact with him.

"Lo siento, coronel, mi amigo dijo que era la mejor que podia hacer," the scientist replies, continuing to try to avoid eye contact.

"Matalo, es un espia americaño," Col. Lins commands as he lifts his hand up as he clenches it into a fist.

"Como desees," the man replies, dropping to a knee before rising back up.

"Ahora que alguien me traiga una bebida de verdad," Col. Lins proclaim as the man stands up, struggling to keep the vial secure in his grasp.

Grabbing hold of the vial, the man shifts over to the scientist and uncorks it before placing it down onto a silver tray. As he watches as the man places the vial into his other hand, he turns to the two guards as they make their way toward the bars. As each grabbed a side of his hand, they pulled his arm out between the bars and lift his sleeve. Holding it up, the scientist takes the vial and approaches Esteban as he begins to clench his fist causing the muscles to tighten.

"No te preocupes, el vodka ruso relaja a todos," the guard says as he tightens his grasp of his arm.

Watching as the man approaches, Esteban stares down the scientist as he dumps the liquid inside the vial out onto the skin around his elbow. Feeling the burn from the alcohol as it falls onto the floor, Esteban continues to watch the scientist as he begins to lift the syringe just above his skin. Taking his first attempt to crack the epidermis, the needle bounces off as Esteban flexes his muscles. With a smirk, the scientist forces himself to turn to the two guards holding his arm in place. Watching as they both nod, he watches as they pull his arm enough to place his body up against the cell bars.

"Let him go," the boy screams, causing the rest of the room to turn to him.

"Tu habla ingles?" Col. Lins asks as the rest of the guards look at the boy. He then turns his attention to the two holding his arms back, nodding his head which sends them forward a couple of steps. Dragging the boy in front of him, he gets feet from Col. Lins who stares into his eyes when he sees something that he never saw before. Pulling his head back, he looks over at Esteban who starts to shake in anger before turning his gaze to the boy.

Catching his attention as it starts to drift toward Esteban, the boy turns to Col. Lins and the smirk that grew on his face.

"Responde la pregunta," the guards say in unison as they tighten their grasp around his wrists. Sending pulses of pain down his arm, the boy drops to his knees before nodding his head to answer the question. Turning his smile to a chuckle, Col. Lins turns to Esteban in time to see his eyes begin to turn red as blood seeps in from the sides. Then with little effort, Esteban twists his arm horizontally before pulling it back to him. As it slides between the bars, the two guards struggling to maintain their grasp slam into the bars, bouncing them off of the frame. Watching pieces of drywall fall from the roof, Esteban turns toward Col. Lins as the rest of the guards start to rush for the open doorway.

"Adelante, pon a tu hijo en peligro," Col. Lins yells as he rips the boy from the grasp of the two guards. Turning their attention to their rifles, they step toward Col. Lins even as the scientist watches from the side with the syringe still in hand. To his amusement, Esteban steps back as the scientist continues to bounce his sight between the two men.

"Que quieres que haga?" the scientist asks as he continues to bounce his eyesight between the two men.

"Obtener mi muestra," Col. Lins replies as he continues to tightly hold the boy around his arm.

Turning toward Esteban, the scientist cautiously takes a step toward the bending bars. Entering the space alongside Esteban's shadow, he stops just inches from the bars until Esteban steps forward.

Sneering as he steps toward, Esteban turns his attention up to the frame to see its instability when he hears the boy scream. Shifting his attention downward, he sees Col. Lins squeezing the boy's arm until it reddens and bruises. Looking up at Col. Lins who responds with a nod, he turns to the scientist as his hand carrying the syringe starts to shake.

"Apresurate," Col. Lins yells.

"Solo damelo y lo hare," Esteban says as he turns his attention to Col. Lins who smirks at his statement. Before he can reply, the scientist turns to meet eyes with Col. Lins who nods with a sneer. Turning back to Esteban who cautiously hands him the syringe. Passing the possession over, the scientist darts over to the control panel as they watch as Esteban brings the syringe closer.

"No seas un heroe Tormenta Cubano," Col. Lins says using his free hand to point down toward the syringe.

Snarling as he turns his attention toward the syringe, he lifts it back up as he places his wrist atop the metal connection between the two bars. Aiming it downward, Esteban looks over at the boy as he continues to lift the syringe higher up.

"No lo hagas, " the boy yells as he struggles to move a muscle from out of Col. Lins's grasp.

"Don't look," Esteban says, stabbing himself in the arm with the syringe just as the boy turns away. To Col. Lins amusement, he grimaces as his arm sits motionless atop the connection. Then as Col. Lins continues to look, Esteban turns his attention back to the syringe that remains stuck inside. Shaking his head, he reaches over and pulls back on the plunger as he watches as it starts to fill up with blood. Feeling the tingling, he looks down just as the last couple of drops fill the last bit of space when he releases his hold. To the excitement of Col. Lins, he pulls out the syringe as a couple of droplets slide down his skin. Turning it upright, he looks over at his blood as it swishes within, he sees the flecks of green and yellow floating around as it starts to emit a reddish glow.

"Ahora entregalo," Col. Lins says as he watches as the scientist steps forward with his hand outward.

CHAPTER 3

Looking over at his hand, he turns to the syringe once more before turning to Col. Lins as he starts to get annoyed.

"Coloquelo aqui por favor," the scientist adds as he picks up a silver tray and places it just on the other side of the cell bars.

"Tengo un mejor plan para esto," Esteban replies when he launches the syringe through the bars as it spins through the air. Before Col. Lins can dodge it, the syringe slices across his cheek before impaling itself into the stone wall behind him. Watching as blood starts to reveal itself, he watches as Col. Lins places his free hand up against the wound before bringing it back down to his face.

"Senor, esta bien?" the scientist asks as watches Esteban's face flush as his eyes catch sight of the blood smear.

"Si, ahora toma la jeringa," Col. Lins replies angrily as he points over to the syringe. He then watches as the scientist rushes over to the spot and starts to tug on the plunger when suddenly it dislodges and lands on the floor. Feeling relieved at the unbroken canister, he reaches down and grabs it before placing it in one of the pockets inside his coat. Once secure, the scientist turn as Col. Lins shifts his attention toward Esteban before remembering the boy in his grasp.

"Guardias," Col. Lins yells as suddenly two men carrying rifles appears from the darkness of the doorframe. Kneeling before him, they rise as Esteban shifts his attention toward him.

"Como Podemos ser de servicio?" the guards as in unison as Col. Lins continues to stare in Esteban's direction. His eyes pulsing blood as the scratch along his cheek drips, he turns his attention to the two men.

"Lleva al nino de regreso a su celda de prisión," Col. Lins says before his lips sputter out some blood that had made its way over. Before Esteban can make a move, he pushes the boy toward the two guards. Trapping his arms behind his back, they shove him toward the doorway as he groans as their grip gets tighter. Hearing the boy's cries of pain, Esteban extends his arms out to his side as he starts to shake with rage. Unleashing an unholy scream, Fire charges up his sternum toward his throat as Col. Lins looks on in amusement. Paying no mind, the two guards continue as with one mighty push, the three exit the room. Leaving the two men and the scientist who stands helpless beside the control panel, Col. Lins turns to him and extends his hand. Nodding with confidence, the man reaches inside his lab coat before pulling out a switch with a red button on the top.

Hesitating for a moment, Esteban turns to Col. Lins who shifts his own attention from the switch toward him.

"Noche nocturna Tormenta Cubano," Col. Lins says with a smile as his thumb presses down the button. Suddenly, rumbling, and vibrating surrounds the trio when the scientist charges toward the open doorway. As he approaches space, Esteban looks up as he starts to see a purplish fog start to excrete from out the vents. Surrounding him, he turns to the bars as he goes to look back to see Col. Lins no longer where he was. Instead, he finds him on the outside of the door along with the scientist.

"Te vencere para siempre," Esteban responds as he delivers a fiery blast from with his throat. As the fire spins outward, the fog extinguishes it rapidly as it fills up the room. Continuing to watch the events unfold, the scientist pulls Col. Lins back before slamming the door shut. Sealing him inside, they see his glowing blue eyes as they intensify behind the aura of purple when suddenly they go out. Hearing a gentle thud, Col. Lins turns toward the scientist before looking at himself. Examining the wound once more, he approaches a mirror and looks at his reflection even as it misses a couple of pieces of glass. Brushing off the dirt from his lab coat and the tropical shirt beneath, Col. Lins smirks as he keeps his focus onto his reflection.

"Ya tak blizko," Col. Lins whispers as he takes off the lab coat and places it on a loose piece of metal along the wall. Sticking out of the cold stone wall, the pipe goes up and follows the base of the roof.

"Que dijiste?" the scientist asks as he watches as Col. Lins shifts his attention in the mirror toward him.

"La mision esta casi completa," Col. Lins replies, turning around to face the man. Nodding his head with some nervousness, he watches as Col. Lins starts to extend out his hand toward the man. Without a question, he reaches deep within the pocket as he pulls out the syringe and hands it over to Col. Lins. Smirking as he looks down upon it, he turns his attention to the scientist as he places it within the pocket of his shirt.

"Vamos a ir a Santa Clara?" the scientist asks as he looks over to the open door at the end of the hallway.

"Si pasaremos a la siguiente fase de la mision," Col. Lins says as he turns around to investigate inside from the blurry window atop of the door. Watching as the fog continues to settle, suddenly a loud vacuum comes on as it starts to return the room to normal. Before long, his evil grin grows as he starts to see the shadow of Esteban's fallen body as it lay on the floor. Unconscious, he remains still to the amusement of Col. Lins as the window muffles out his laughter. Placing his hands against the stone wall around the door, his hands start to leave an imprint as pebbles fall to the floor.

"Cual es la mision de nuevo?" the scientist asks as the smirk on Col. Lins's face goes away. Anger replacing the amusement, his bloodshot eyes turn down as his muscles start to shake. He then watches as the stones start to crack from the force of his hands.

"No es tu problema," Col. Lins replies as suddenly his hand caves the large stone. Before the man can move, Col. Lins turn around and strikes the man across the face with it as he releases the rock on impact. Sending it flying into the wall, the rock explodes just as the scientist crumbles to the floor. As the pebbles land on his chest, Col. Lins smiles as he sees the scientist struggling to breathe. At the man's side, Col. Lins's lab coat shifts from white to red as blood from the man's wound fills up the fabric. Chuckling at the results of his action, he extends his arms out as the power inside of him begins to control him. Seducing every brain cell, Col. Lins tightens his hands into fists as he watches as the veins along his arms start to pop to the surface.

"Lo que le sucedio?" a voice rings out, causing Col. Lins to drop the remnants of the stone before lowering his smile into a frown. Turning his attention, he sees one of the guards' charges forward before kneeling beside the fallen scientist. Watching as he checks for a heartbeat, he looks up at Col. Lins, who shakes his head.

"El heroe hizo esto," Col. Lins replies as he looks out toward the window, hiding the smirk. Watching as he charges toward the window to see the unconscious Tormenta Cubano, the guard turns his attention back to Col. Lins as his hands tighten around the rifle.

"Terminemos con el," the guard says as Col. Lins momentarily investigates the room before turning back to the guard. Shaking his head, he places his hand onto the man's shoulder as he backs away from the window.

"El todavia tiene la pieza que falta a nuestra misión," Col. Lins replies as the guard nods. Watching as he relaxes his hand away from the rifle, Col. Lins moves toward the fallen scientist.

"Entonces, ¿qué le dire a los otros hombres?" the guard asks as he watches Col. Lins kneel beside the scientist.

"Para vigilar al chico mientras me dirijo nuestra base cerca La Campana," Col. Lins replies as he turns his sight onto his fallen comrade.

Without a reply, the guard bows before heading back down the hallway toward a spiral suitcase. With each clanging step, the man gets farther away as it once more leaves Col. Lins alone. Shifting his attention toward the man, he strikes him in the chest with a smirk before rising back to his feet. Standing once again, he softly chuckles before turning back toward another open doorway. His eyes then shift down to the pocket of his tropical shirt. Placing his hand atop the pocket, his eyes widen as he looks down to see no trace of the syringe. Checking all his pockets thoroughly, he flaps his shirt about without a sign. As his eyes dart around the room in search of the syringe, gurgling sounds send his eyes downward.

"Que has hecho?" Col. Lins asks as he turns and kneels beside the scientist.

"He vencido a los todopoderosos Col. Lins," the scientist chuckles as blood bubbles up from between his lips.

"Donde esta la jeringa?" Col. Lins asks angrily as he begins to shake the scientist who continues gurgling between laughs. After beginning to shake him violently, the man passes out until Col. Lins screams into his face. Arising the man from unconsciousness, he then starts to shake him once more in search of answers.

"Lejos de aqui," the scientist mutters as his eyes shut before Col. Lins slams him down.

Realizing the guard has had it, Col. Lins charges down the hall toward the staircase as he runs down, leaving the half-conscious man alone in the darkening hallway.

"Se ha ido?" a voice asks.

"Si," the scientist replies as he keeps his eyes shut. After a couple more seconds, a shadow creeps inside through the darkness. Shifting between rows of light, the figure reveals himself to be a man in a hood. His features hidden from the light, the person kneels beside the fallen scientist. Struggling to move his hands, he motions over to his far side. As the man shifts around him, he picks him up to reveal the syringe hiding underneath his bloody lab coat. Grabbing hold of it, he places the man back down before getting back to his feet.

"Adios Viejo amigo," the man replies as he turns his attention to the window after watching the scientist take his final breath. Looking within, the man watches as Esteban remains on the floor of the cage. With a smirk, he starts to reach for the door handle when he starts to hear the growing sounds of footsteps. Turning it with little hesitation, he sneaks inside the room just as the vacuum shuts off. Plotting an escape, he shifts his body out of sight of the window when he hears the footstep coming even closer. Then after a couple of seconds they stop as he can hear a faint laugh coming from the scientist. Gurgling between each round, a shadow grows beneath the door and the floor.

"Has mentido por última vez," a deep voice bellows. With that, the laughter ceases as another loud crack rings out.

Feeling his breath quicken, the man squeezes himself up against the wall as he hears another set of footsteps. Hearing them stop, the glass of the window starts to bend from the force of the man's hand when suddenly the doorknob starts to move. As the opening is about to reveal the hiding man, the door stops moving as suddenly another round of footsteps approaches from the distance. Growing louder with each passing second, the steps make their way down the hallway as the door shuts on their arrival. Feeling things calm within his body, the weight on the door lessens as he hears the man shift his breathing.

"Coronel Lins lo que le ha pasado?" a strange voice asks.

"La Tormenta Cubano lo ataco," Col. Lins replies after a few moments of silence.

"Si esta libre, debes largarte de aquí," the other voice says.

"Debemos traer al prisonero antes de que lo encuentre," Col. Lins replies.

"Te lo traere en el yate," the other voice replies.

"Voy a estar esperando," Col. Lins says.

"Deberia hacer sonar la alarma?" the other voice asks.

"No, dejame el heroe a mi," Col. Lins replies when the man hears cracking knuckles.

"Como usted ordena," the other voice says when suddenly the sound of rapid footsteps head away from the door. Disappearing into silence, they fade away as once more nothing is heard beyond the sound of breathing.

Hearing nothing, the man in the room pokes his head out into the window, catching sight of Col. Lins as he kneels beside the fallen scientist. Reaching down, he picks up the bloody lab coat and sneers as he gets back to feet. Turning toward the fallen man, he throws the coat overtop his head as it lands softly. Covering the man's head, Col. Lins swiftly looks toward the door once more as the man is just able to dodge his gaze. After a couple of moments, footsteps once more echo about, allowing the man inside to motion back to the window. Seeing no trace of Col. Lins as the steps grow fainter, he turns his attention to Esteban.

The man then cautiously opens the cage door as the bars bend ever so slightly. Getting closer, the man approaches him as he drops his hood. Revealing his lighter skin tone along with his light brown hair that covers his shoulders, the man unzips the jacket as it reveals various bars of colors. Approaching with a stern caution, the man kneels beside Esteban and pulls out the syringe in his pocket. Attempting to inject him, the man suddenly realizes that during the various trips of transportation the needle had fallen. Shaking his head, he places Esteban upward as he shifts his sight toward a cabinet with a single drawer ajar. Rushing over, he finds himself face to face with various boxes when he sees the word, "agujas" written along one of them.

Pulling it down, the man takes one out, and unwraps it before placing it onto the opening of the syringe. After releasing the air bubbles within, he turns to Esteban's body as it remains still.

"Vuelve a la pelea," the man whispers when he leans back before stabbing Esteban in the torso. As the needle punctures the skin, it was like a bolt of lightning shot up his body as suddenly his eyes wake from behind their eye lids. Watching as Esteban comes into consciousness, the man turns his attention to the syringe before pushing down on the plunger. As the radiating blood sinks down into Esteban's body, the glowing blood continues to make its way through his chest toward the rest of his body. His muscles tightening as air fills his lungs, Esteban's bloodshot eyes turn to the man.

"Donde esta mi hijo?" Esteban asks softly as he looks around the room seeing no other person.

"Lo encontraremos," the man replies as he stands up before offering his hand to Esteban.

With a nod, Esteban grabs hold as the man pulls him up from the ground as his balance starts to recover. Wobbling at first, Esteban stabilizes as he looks once more around the room. Regaining his breath along with his strength, Esteban takes a couple of steps toward the open cage door. Suddenly he takes a stumble, yet just as he is about to lose his balance he grabs hold of the doorframe. Secure around the bar, Esteban stands up straight and takes a couple of deep breaths. Shaking his head free of doubt, Esteban takes a pair of steps out of the cage. Turning back toward the man, he sees him smirk as he makes his way out alongside him.

"Como me encontraste?" Esteban asks as the man finishes stepping from the cage.

"Segui el olor del café Cubano," the man replies with a smile, watching as the color in Esteban's skin starts to return.

"En serio?" Esteban asks, smelling his dusty shirt as tries to avoid the spots of blood spatter.

"No, las segue desde la vieja plaza hasta aquí," the man replies as he chuckles watching Esteban lower his shirt.

Shaking his head as he looks around at the flashing lights and shiny metal cage bars, he feels a sensation going down his shirt. Looking down, he sees a trail of blood oozing from the injection site toward his stomach. Turning his attention toward the man he places his hand on the site. "Mario, Necesito un vendaje."

Nodding his head, Mario turns his attention toward the cabinets and drawers beside the panel of switches. Making his way over, he searches the drawers first when after getting to the final one he finds one. Pulling it free from the drawer and unwrapping it, Mario watches as Esteban pulls down his shirt to reveal the bloody wound.

Momentarily turning his attention back to the drawer, he opens the container as a spiraling mist rises from the opening. Reaching in, the man pulls out a small container with a swirling clear liquid laying within. Smirking, he closes the container back up before turning his attention toward Esteban as he continues to watch the blood dribble down.

"Que es eso?" Esteban asks as he watches as Mario approaches as he uncorks the container.

"No preguntes," Mario replies as he stops just inches from the wound. Without hesitation, he dumps the liquid onto his arm causing Esteban to grit his teeth and tighten his muscles. Throwing down the vial, allowing it to shatter along the floor, he slaps the bandage onto the skin and secures it to the wound. Stopping the blood, Mario steps back as he watches Esteban pat down the area.

"¿Ahora, donde está mi hijo?" Esteban asks as he turns his focus to Mario who stares back in silence.

"El esta en algun lugar de esta torre," Mario replies as he watches as Esteban clenches his jaw as his anger intensifies. Without an answer, Mario watches as Esteban charges out of the doorway. Turning the corner as his shadow disappears, Mario heads behind him only to see him frozen beside the fallen scientist. With his hand on the bloody lab coat, Mario watches Esteban as he places it back before turning his attention down the hall. Getting up from the ground, he angrily turns away from Mario before delivering a punch to the side. Causing the rocks to pebble along with the shards of drywall, he stands still as Mario approaches him peacefully.

"Col. Lins va a pagar," Esteban mutters as Mario looks down at the scrapes along his knuckles. Tiny specks of blood sliding down his skin, Mario turns his attention toward his face when he starts to make his way down the hall.

"Sabes a donde vas?" Mario asks, freezing Esteban in his tracks a few feet away.

"Voy a donde sea que lo mantengan," Esteban replies as he starts to pan around the hall looking for a sign. Then before Mario can reply, Esteban hears a pair of chuckles coming from far off which sends his attention in the direction. Without a word, he takes off with a blaze as it leaves Mario alone in the hall, shrugging his shoulders.

As the ground settles, Mario looks over at the fallen scientist and after nodding his head he heads down in the direction. Running at normal speed, Mario turns the corner as he sees Esteban stuck in a fork in the hall. Then just as he arrives, Esteban looks back at him before cracking his knuckles. Once the final joint loosens he takes off down the left pathway, and into a lit room at the other end. Hearing no screams of anguish, Mario makes his approach as he hears shattering wood. Upon his arrival, he stops in the doorway trying to catch his breath when he sees Esteban standing in the center. With a massive window behind him, lightning cracks along the horizon which brings the sound of thunder. As the reverberations die down, he squats in the center as he admires the broken shards of a pair of chairs all over the floor. Meanwhile, along the wall to his right are the remains of a metal table. Scattering along the floor, Mario makes his way through the ruins as he looks over Esteban.

"Escuche risas," Esteban mutters as he looks around the room.

"Bueno yo no veo a nadie," Mario says with his arms spread out.

Esteban looks around in disgust before turning his attention to Mario who steps forward as once again he extends his hand. With a smirk, he gets to his feet when he starts to stumble a couple of steps. Struggling to stay upright, he leans on Mario who struggles to hold him up. As Mario looks around the room seeing the space around him, he finds an old metal chair hiding beneath a counter space just to their left. Carefully making their way toward it, Mario feels Esteban shift his weight off, allowing him to reach for the chair to unfold it. Placing it steady on the ground away from the debris, he watches as Esteban sits down as he struggles to catch his breath.

"Cuanta sangre te sacaron?" Mario asks as he places his hand on his friend's shoulder.

"Perdi la cuenta," Esteban replies as he pulls up his sleeves, revealing the countless injection sites and the numerous bruises.

Shaking his head in anger, he looks around when among a couple piles of paper, he sees a tiny Styrofoam cup along with a stack of tiny paper cups. Grinning, he walks over and grabs it as Esteban looks over, trying to figure out what his friend is doing. Turning around, Mario watches as Esteban's expression changes as his nostrils flare with the arrival of this familiar scent.

"Justo el impulse que necesitas," Mario says with a smile as he undoes the top of the cup and places it gently into one of the smaller cups.

"Seguro que tenemos tiempo para esto?" Esteban asks as he grabs hold of the cup with a shaky hand. Struggling to not spill it, he brings it up to his lips as with one swift gulp, the brown liquid is down his throat.

"Segun tu apariencia, es possible que necesitas una dosis doble," Mario replies taking the small cup back from Esteban. Watching as his grasp steadies, Esteban looks back in confusion.

"Es tan malo?" Esteban asks as he watches as Mario pours another shot of cafecito.

"Eres tan blanco como ese científico de ahí atrás," Mario replies as he hands Esteban the cup back as the liquid inside sways about.

"Siempre has tenido facilidad con las palabras," Esteban says, raising the shot to his friend before pouring it down his throat. Gulping down the remnants, he wipes the residue from his face when he starts to feel his muscle tighten. Feeling his heartbeat speed up and his strength returning, Esteban sits back in the chair as Mario watches the metal back bend further. With each breath, Esteban's power return as he feels the caffeine cause the blood to rush through his arteries. Restoring his energy, Esteban looks down at the cup before handing it back to Mario who takes a shot himself. As the two men enjoy a cheery moment, Esteban's smile fades as he heads toward the massive glass window along the back wall. From roof to floor, the blinds covering the window split open with Esteban's touch.

Revealing the outside world which he had only seen in his dreams, his heart sinks seeing the ruins that make up the land of his birth. Gone were the fruit trees and traditional architecture, and in their place were fields of dirt with craters from various explosives. He wasn't home instead it was an old submarine base from which Esteban had known from his lifetime once before. Stories below him, Cuban soldiers patrol the grounds along with Humvees as helicopters sound from above. Feeling enough of the depression and despair, Esteban turns back when suddenly he hears approaching footsteps.

"Que es?" Mario asks as he turns to the doorway as Esteban rises from the chair before kicking it through the wall. Sending shards of drywall onto the floor, Mario steps back toward Esteban as the footsteps get louder. With each passing moment, they continue to get closer when suddenly a pair of guards appear with red beams aiming at the two men. Soon ten men come inside as they line up from left to right as they completely block the doorway. Continuing to watch as the men get into place, Mario drops the co.

"Baja tus armas," Esteban yells as he watches as the guards turn their heads to one another before looking back at him and Mario.

"Buen intento," Mario whispers when they both turn as from out of the darkness, sounds of clapping echo about. As they stand in suspense, they watch as from out of the hallway appears Col. Lins with a grin from ear to ear. Still clapping even as he makes his way through the doorway, he stops behind the line of guns when he places his hands back along his side.

"Bueno veo que todavia te queda un amigo," Col. Lins laughs before the group of guards unlock their weapons before placing their fingers on the triggers. Standing still, Mario and Esteban look at one another as red dots appear on their bodies before they turn their attention back to Col. Lins.

"Solo dinos donde está el niño y nadie sale lastimado," Mario says as Esteban continues to look on in silence.

"Tengo tanto miedo de un héroe roto y su compañero humaño,"

Col. Lins laughs as the rest of the guards remain silent.

"Si deberías," Esteban replies as his eyes redden with flames as they slink through his chest and neck. Before either of them can make a move, one of the guards fires their gun as a dart spins through the air as the blue feathers catch Mario's eyes.

"Cuidado," Mario yells as he shields Esteban when he feels the prick into his back. Stumbling as his vision blurs instantly, Mario places his hands onto Esteban's chest before turning himself around.

"Derribalos," Col. Lins screams as he points toward the two men as they prepare to fire the next round.

"Los detendre, asi que ve a buscar a tu hijo," Mario replies before charging at the group causing them to momentarily lower their weapons. Then as they continue to watch, he slides down onto the ground as he picks up a couple of metal bars from the broken chairs that broke during Esteban's rage. With one in each hand, Mario javelins them into the chest of two guards causing them to fall back as their fingers press down on the trigger. Sending darts into the roof above, Mario charges toward the others as they start to try to pin him down. Blow after blow, Mario knocks three down until finally the numbers get to him. Continuing to struggle, he turns toward Esteban seeing the conflict in his eyes.

His fists clenching tighter, Mario shakes him off before stepping on the men's feet as it causes them to release their grasp. Once loose, he turns around with his fist out in front when he connects with their jaws, sending them spiraling toward the ground. With two men left as Col. Lins remain behind them, Mario watches as Col. Lins smirks when suddenly the sound of another shot being fired rings out. Seconds later, Mario feels another pinch along his neck which causes him to stumble more as it continues to blur his vision.

"SAL" Mario yells as he charges the remaining duo.

Gulping down his feelings, Esteban turns toward the window and with one swift charge, jumps through the window causing the glass to rain down below. Leaping into the darkness, Esteban flies before coming to a stop as he turns back to see his friend as he catches sight of two more rounds of smoke coming from the guards' weapons. Watching as they jump on top of him, Esteban struggles to deliberate his next move until suddenly the spotlight from the nearby guard tower catches him in mid-air. Shifting his attention, he flies into the cloudy sky above as the sounds of machine gun fire break the silence. Disappearing into the streaks of the star light, he lands safely along the rooftop as he watches as the spotlight loses track.

After a couple of moments, Esteban's hands slam into the cement railing along the roof. Feeling a numbness rise from his wrists as his knees start to tremble. Looking around as the spotlight disappears, his sight starts to blur as he stumbles about. Dropping to his knees after stumbling about, he runs his hands over the bare skin of his neck. That is when he felt it sticking out of the side, the dart impaling itself into him as the feathery ending ran through his fingers.

"Esos bastardos," Esteban mutters as his face slams into the ground. Watching as the moonlight fades away, his eyes shut as darkness starts to take over.

Meanwhile within the building, Col. Lins stands in front of the broken window frame. Looking all around for any sign, he watches as the spotlight turns off. Angrily, he stares at the broken shards of glass along the ground, he then turns around to the guards as they stand in front of the doorway.

"Teniente coronel, Adelante," Col. Lins yells as one of the men behind the guards' steps forward.

With no response, the man lowers his head as he makes his way to Col. Lins' side. Upon his arrival, Col. Lins places his arm around the lieutenant and brings him toward the edge of the window frame. Carefully avoiding the broken shards of glass protruding from the metal frame, the two men stare out into the night world.

"Como escapo?" Col. Lins asks as he pulls the man closer to him.

"Lo golpe Col. Lins," the man replies as he points down at the specks of shining blood as they head toward the opening.

Col. Lins sneers as he shakes his head as the man gulps down some saliva, watching as Col. Lins looks down at the ruble before turning back to the man beside him.

"Sin embargo, él no se encuentra en ninguna parte," Col. Lins says as his eyes redden with anger.

"El no recibirá su pecado," the man replies as he tries to take a small step back from the edge. Replying with a sneer, Col. Lins suddenly shoves the man over the edge as he screams all the way down. After hearing things go silent, Col. Lins turn back to the group that look on in shock. Without saying a word, he   makes his way toward them as they look in silence. Splitting the group, he heads toward the open doorway as the rest of the group shift their attention opposite the broken window. Still recovering from their wounds, the guards angrily make their way forward as Mario remains unconscious. Dragging his lifeless body toward the end of the hall, the group turns as Col. Lins approaches an elevator before pressing the button along the wall.

After hearing the click, the light around the down arrow turns red as they hear the movement within the chamber. After a couple of moments, the doors open to reveal an empty space as Col. Lins steps to the side to allow the others within. Watching as Mario remains in the center of the elevator, Col. Lins makes his way to the front of the group. Turning his head toward a guard, he nods as he watches the man press the bottom button.

With a single push, the door screeches to a shut as suddenly the elevator drops into the shaft. As they wait for the doors to reopen, Mario releases a groan as the two guards beside him tighten their hands into fists.

"No pierdas tu tiempo," Col. Lins says as he turns around and reaches into the guard's holster. Pulling the gun free, he aims it toward Mario's neck and fires a shot. Unleashing a deafening sound, the guards grimace as Mario's face drops into his chest. As the smoke dissipates from the barrel, Col. Lins turns around to face the door once more with his arms crossing in front of him. With the gun in front of his waist, he watches as the movement stops. A few seconds later, the door opens to reveal a dark hall. With cement and stone going as far as their eyesight allows, Col. Lins throws the gun down the hall. Hearing the echo lead to silence, he motions two fingers forward as a pair of guards lead the way.

With guns at the ready, the guards led the way as Col. Lins watches with focus and intent. Hearing no gunfire, Col. Lins sneers as he sends the rest of the group forward. Watching as they drag Mario's lifeless body into the darkness, Col. Lins smirks as he follows in the back of the pack. Entering the shadows one by one, they step within which reveals a closed door standing in their way. Coming to a stop, Col. Lins motions one of the men forward as he watches him grab hold of the doorknob. Then with a flick of the wrist, the door pops open as it reveals a faintly lit room. Once inside, they step into a room containing four prison cells made of rusty metal bars. Pushing their way forward, the group steps inside as they approach an open cell on the left.

With no words, Col. Lins watches as the men step inside with Mario still unconscious. Placing him down along a metal makeshift bed frame, they turn back around and exit as they close the door behind them. Making their way toward the open doorway, Col. Lins approaches the cage and grabs hold of a pair of bars. With little effort, the bars bend and creak as he watches Mario barely breathing along the cement floor. Beginning to chuckle, he turns his attention to the cage beside it. Backing away from the cage as he approaches the other cell, Col. Lins sneers as he walks past the occupant within. Within was none other than Esteban's son as he looks back helpless.

A mix of blood and tears covering his entire face, Esteban's son looks on with sadness as he watches Col. Lins make his way past the bars.

"What have you done to my dad?" the boy asks as he weakly makes his way to his feet. Struggling to maintain his balance, he turns to Col. Lins as he watches him freeze in the middle of a step.

"Tu padre esta muerto," Col. Lins says with a laugh as he watches the boy turn his head before looking at the man beside him.

"I'm sorry what did you say my Spanish isn't good," the boy replies, silencing Col. Lins.

"Your father is dead," Col. Lins says with a chuckle as he watches the boy's face grow paler than before. Watching as his eyes produce a fresh batch of tears, Col. Lins watches as they zig zag past his cheeks toward his chin. As they drip down to the cold ground below, Col. Lins continues to laugh as he steps back from the cage bars.

Anger taking the place of despair, the boy makes his way forward as he watches Col. Lins maintain his stature. Then with all the anger he can muster, he grabs the bars and starts to shake them as he unleashes a primordial scream. Echoing off the empty room, it is ignored as Col. Lins continues to chuckle in response. Keeping his balance up against the bars, he watches as Col. Lins steps toward the bars as he remains just out of reach of the boy's grasp. Out of frustration, the boy unlocks his hand from the bar and sticks it between two of the bars before taking swipes at the air. After a couple of rounds, Col. Lins grabs hold of his wrist before squeezing it tight.

"Like father, like son," Col. Lins mutters as he pushes the boy's arm back between the bars, which causes him to take a couple of steps back.

Staring a hole back at him, the boy massages his wrist as he watches Col. Lins take a couple of steps toward the doorway.

Then as he shifts his weight, Col. Lins freezes momentarily before lifting a hand over his mouth as he starts to deal with a coughing fit. Feeling his face starting to flush, he calms it down as he looks over toward the open doorway, seeing a shadow approach through the dim light.

"Coronel, estas bien?" a voice says from the darkness.

"Necesito una bebida con cafeina," Col. Lins replies as he tries to fight off the coughing episode.

"Pero señor, este es el quinto en una hora," the voice replies.

"Bueno, consígueme las cosas más fuertas de los fuentes entonces," Col. Lins replies angrily as he makes his way toward the doorway. Stepping through the darkness, leaving no sign but the fading sounds of his coughing, the boy turns to Mario, who remains still along the floor.

Making his way toward the metal bedframe, he continues to look over at Mario when suddenly the door slams shut. Allowing the faint light to shine along the fading metal of the doorknob, the boy shifts toward the door when he starts to hear some rustling from beside him. Turning his attention, he sees Mario starting to regain consciousness as he starts to look around the room. Taking in his surroundings, he pulls the dart out of his neck before bringing it toward his eyes.

29

CHAPTER 4

Disgusted, he lobs the dart out of his cell as it lands harmlessly beside the wall between the two sets of cells. Then without a word, Mario turns to the cell beside him when he sees the boy sitting with eyes as wide as saucers.

"Are you ok?" the boy asks as he sits back on the metal bedframe. Keeping his attention on Mario, he watches him nod carefully. Watching as Mario starts to shake the paralysis out of his fingers, he turns to the boy who continues to watch him.

"What does he mean like father like son?" Mario asks with a thick Spanish accent.

"Esteban is my father, or I should say was," the boy replies as he starts to sulk his head down into his hands as they lay on his lap.

"Cuál es tu nombre?" Mario asks as he watches as the boy momentarily gives him the side eye before closing them back up. After keeping silent for a few seconds beside a gentle whimper, Mario starts to think how to translate it into English.

"Rafael Morales," the boy mumbles as he wipes the tears from off his face.

Realizing that the boy was none other than the son that Esteban was searching for, Mario increases his efforts to break free from the dart's effect. Resorting to slamming his hand down onto the metal frame, Mario turns to the boy who shifts his own sight toward him.

"Your father is not dead," Mario says as he continues to shake the feeling back into his hand.

Hearing those words, a glimmer of light enters the boy's eyes as he turns to Mario who gets up from the metal. Struggling to maintain his balance, he carefully takes a couple of steps toward the bars that separate the two cells.

"But he said he is," the boy replies as he starts to lift his head.

"Como se dice he is lying in English?" Mario says as he watches the boy ball up his hands into fists.

"So, where is he?" the boy asks.

"He is searching for you," Mario replies as he starts to inspect the room around the room.

"Ok and who are you?" the boy asks as he tries to wipe away the remnants of old tears from his skin.

"My name is Mario, I am like a brother to your father," Mario replies.

"Este voz--Esa es Manzana Loca?" a voice calls out from the other side of the room. Shifting their attention toward the cells, Mario watches as from out of the streaks of dim light, a man in a pair of torn fatigue pants steps forward before placing his hands around the bars.

"Ese era yo hace mucho tiempo," Mario replies as he takes a couple of steps toward the man. Getting closer he starts to see traits resembling a man he had seen long ago. From his graying brown hair to his blue eyes that have sunk in over time, Mario continues to inspect the man as he tries to place a name to the body.

"No te acuerdas de mi?" the man asks as Mario continues to look over at him.

"Pareces familiar, pero ha pasado tanto tiempo," Mario replies as the man places his head up against the bars.

"Soy yo Randolf, tu viejo compañero de literas," the man replies before picking his head up.

Seeing him speak, Rafael turns to the cage in the direction of Mario's attention and sees nothing. Just darkness and shadows, he turns back to Mario as his eyes refuse to blink as he remains frozen. Meanwhile before Mario, the man before him starts to grin as he extends his arms out from the cage.

"Estas muerto," Mario yells as the man begins to chuckle when he steps through the bars. Remaining silent, he walks closer to Mario's cage which causes him to retreat a couple steps.

"Podrias haberme ayudado," the man screams as blood starts to slide down his chest from various spots.

With his eyes wide, Mario shakes his head as the image of the man fades from view. Returning the scene back to normal, he wipes the sliding drops of sweat from his face. Struggling to regain his breath, he sits back down on the metal bedframe before turning his attention to Rafael.

"No debi haber venido aqui," Mario mumbles as he looks down at his lap.

"What is happening?" Rafael asks as he watches Mario shift his attention back to him.

"Even heroes have demons in their past," Mario replies, looking over at the empty cage once more.

"Wait, my dad is a hero?" Rafael asks, causing Mario to break his stare before returning his attention toward the boy.

"Your dad is not just a hero, he is a superhero," Mario replies, watching as the boy's eyes light up in shock.

"Does my dad have superpowers?" Rafael asks, thinking about all the heroes about whom he had heard. Without a reply, Rafael watches as suddenly Mario turns to the stone wall behind him. Then with no hesitation, he punches a hole through the wall before pulling his hand out. Leaving an enormous hole in the wall, Mario looks down at his hand, seeing the shards of stone and drywall laying in the cracks of his fingers.

"That is just a sample of the powers your father possesses," Mario replies, wiping the debris from his hand, watching as it piles up on the ground.

"Wait, so how did you guys get powers?" Rafael asks as he sits down.

"That is a long story that goes back many decades ago," Mario replies.

"Well, we have nowhere to go," Rafael adds as he sits back on the bed frame, placing himself up against the wall.

"Very true so let me get started," Mario says as he takes a deep breath.

Some stories start simple and yet transition into chaos. From farm hand to soldier with a twist and turn through heroics. Your father Esteban was born and raised in Santa Clara, which is the capital of Villa Clara. It has undergone some change through the years yet on the outskirts exist rural farms. Growing everything from mangoes to plaintains, agriculture is a large foundation for those who live within the city. Yet during times like these things have gotten rough which has brought forth various chapters in Cuba's history. To be more precise around the time of October in 1962, Cuba was walking a fine line between tranquility and war. This is around the time where the story of your father and I's lives changes forever.

See as a young man, Esteban Martinez grew up along the rural areas of town, growing plants alongside his family. Then once they passed in age, he took over and began working along the rows of trees helping to keep the farm in prosperity. Yet one day as the sun was in its trek through the sky, Esteban takes his first step out of his property and into a new day. Step after step, he makes his way through the creaking patio boards when he makes his way onto the dirt path leading from the farm. Into the blazing sun, his eyes squint as he makes the turn toward his fruiting trees as they sit along the soil. With a smile, he makes his way as occasionally a cloud will drift overhead. Allowing him a moment of shade, Esteban breathes easily as it blows over, bringing the sun back from hiding. Then after a couple of moments, he steps into the shadow of the shade trees before him. Spotting his warping wooden bucket, he bends down to pick it up and places a faded hat upon his head.

"Necesita ayuda hoy?" I ask which turns his attention toward a pair of trees. I watch as his eyes meet mine as I place my hand upon the trunk of the nearby banana tree .

"Estas Seguro de que no quieres ser perezoso hoy?" Esteban replies with a smirk as he tosses the bucket at me. Catching it, I check my hands for splinters as I grab the handle which lowers the bottom of it toward the ground.

"Ahora se amable con tu mejor amigo en toda Cuba," I reply with a sarcastic grin as I watch him pick up another bucket that sat just beside the base of a nearby tree.

"Bueno, para ser justos, mis opciones son limitadas," Esteban replies as he looks around the trees surrounding us.

"Ja Ha muy divertido," I reply, shaking my head as I make my way closer before punching him in the shoulder. Turning my attention toward a nearby tree, my eyes drift upward as I see a hand of bananas swaying above. As its shadow drifts back and forth, I turn toward the stalk before turning my attention in search of something. Hearing Esteban's chuckle, I shift my attention toward him as he looks up at the fruit hanging overhead.

"Te estas perdiendo algo?" Esteban asks as his mood calms.

"Una escalera seria agradable," I reply as I motion my hand upward toward the top of the tree. Without a word, he smirks as he points in my direction which shifts my attention. Seeing nothing at first, I look around the other side when my eyes catch sight of a strange shadow along the sandy dirt. Then there it was leaning against the layers of stalk, a wooden ladder with its rails digging themselves into the ground. Snarling, I grab it from the ground and place it on the opposite side of the tree as it steadies a few feet over our head.

"Lo hiciste todo por ti mismo," Esteban says as he chuckles before placing his back up against the base of another tree. Watching me as I head up the ladder step by step, I approach the bananas as my hand sways just beneath them. Then after taking another step upward, my hands grab hold of the stalk and rips them down as they free from the tree. Receiving an ovation from Esteban assumably in sarcasm, I make my way back to the ground as the bananas hang off the edge of the rail.

Now usually our day would continue with me making my way down before placing the bananas into the basket. Then one by one we would usually continue until we have completely gotten all the ripe ones. However, this day took a turn as I got within a pair of steps from the ground. Just as my foot is about to lift off the step, a plane zooms overhead shaking the ladder with its acceleration. My hands holding firm, the ladder steadies when suddenly a bunch of planes similar in size thrust past us. Feeling the wobbling, my eyes shut as my grip tightens along the rails of the ladder. Once the sound of them passes, my eyes reopen as the ladder stabilizes.

"Cuales fueron esos?" Esteban says, which causes me to scurry down toward the ground.

"Aviones militares," I reply as I drop the bananas into the basket with an unsteady hand. As my nerves struggle to recover, my eyes look back up into the sky as I still hear the ringing in my ears. Before we can continue, the sounds of a helicopter approach from behind us as it flies overhead. Once we attempt to move on to the next tree, engines start to roar as tires squeal down the road. Shifting our focus, we drop the bucket beside the ladder before turning our attention toward the road that goes along the farm. Sneaking between a pair of trees, Esteban and I make our way toward the ditch beside the road.

Just as our feet get along the slope, the Jeeps approach from the opposite direction. Getting closer, their camo coloring blends with the landscape as they continue to make their way closer. Sending up plumes of exhaust, the vehicles head in our direction until they start to creep toward us as their engines struggle to enter idle even as we stand at the side of the road.

"Me pregunto de que se trata esto," Esteban asks as he turns toward me as my eyes maintain sight of the vehicles closing in. Coming to a stop right in front of us, we step back as both the passenger and side door open. Before us, two men step outside in green and red uniforms. With their caps hanging down at their side, the two place them back on their heads as they approach us. Keeping their icy blue eyes aiming at our faces, the two turn toward each other as one reaches deep within his pockets. Pulling out a folding piece of paper, the man then opens it up before showing the other man who nods in response.

"Podemos ayudarte?" I ask as the two men shift their gaze onto me before spreading it evenly between Esteban and me.

"Skazite im, chto oni pridut s nami, chtoby pomoch nashey missia," one of the men say as they turn to the one with paper in hand. As the other nods as we try to understand what he is saying, we watch as the man turns toward us.

"El general dice que necesita que te unas a la defense de tu pais," the man says to us as we look at each other before turning back. Now it was here that we should have known that we truly had no choice. For you see, we had no option and we had made the biggest mistake of our lives up to this point running toward the street. Had we stayed picking bananas then we could have avoided this entire mess to begin with. As we deliberated our decision, the tall, Russian man pulls a gun on us, causing us to lift our hands to the sky. Then as he held us up, the other man cautiously opens the back door of the Humvee.

Stepping to the side, the man motions the gun toward the open door as we take a deep breath. Slowly we make our way to the opening and then go inside to find two others. Scared and worried, they turn to us as we squeeze into the backseat before the door slams behind us. Encasing us in darkness, our eyes dart around to no avail when I look over at Esteban who is staring out the window in the mist of silence. Before long, the two men make their way around and sit down in the front seats. Once they were in, the doors slam which shakes the suspension of the Humvee. As I went to speak, the engine starts to rev as the man puts his foot on the gas causing the car start to move.

Turning my attention to Esteban, I watch as he continues to stare back at his farm as it falls off into the horizon. Turning his gaze, I watch as his face remains stoic as a mix of anger and fear fills his eyes. Watching as he squeezes his hands into fists, I nudge his arm, causing his attention to shift to me. Nodding my head, he takes a couple of deep breaths after looking out the glass window once more. See, Esteban was like a brother to me, and I could not let him get in any trouble. Seeing him calm, I turn to the others as they sulk in their seat with their heads in their lap.

"Cuanto tiempo llevas aqui?" I ask them as the road starts to get bumpy. I watch as they lift their heads up from their hands as tears fall from their cheeks.

"Se siente como una eternidad," one of the men mutter out as they struggle to wipe away some of the tears. Trying to keep their composure, the two console one another when suddenly my attention shifts to one of the soldiers up front as he turns back.

"Mantengalo allo abajo," the soldier yells as the two men cower in fear before he turns his gaze onto me.

"O que?" I reply rebelliously when suddenly I hear the brakes come to a squealing halt. Jerking to a stop, the driver pulls his gun and aims it in my face, so close in fact I can smell the fresh gun powder as it leaches from the nozzle. Placing his finger on the trigger, he looks at me with a smirk.

"Mueres," the man yells as his face reddens with anger. Then just as he starts to pull the trigger, the other soldier beside him turns toward him and places his hand on top of the gun and lowers it down. Watching as the two men look at one another, I feel a nudge on the side of my arm, which causes me to turn to Esteban.

"Su dereza sera quebrantada en el tiempo," the soldier whispers as the other relaxes the tension in his hand. Taking a deep breath, the man places the gun back into its holster before turning his attention back toward the wheel. With some pressure on the pedal, the car resumes its motion as the other soldier turns his attention toward me and Esteban.

"Nos vas a dejar ir?" I ask only to see him pointing out the window with a devilish grin. Turning my attention along with Esteban, we see as it was no longer the area around our farm instead the entrance to a wooden camp. Walls as high as palms with guards posting all around, my eyes look back to see nothing but burnt ground and fresh cinders sprouting embers.

"Ustedes son aprendices ahora," the man says as he chuckles before turning back around.

Leaving us in turmoil, I hear the somber cries from the two men beside me as I try to sneak a peek past Esteban, who remains with his hand on top of the cloth texture surrounding us. Then before anyone can speak, the car comes to a stop beside the entrance of the camp as a pair of guards in green and red uniforms approach the Humvee. Guns in hand, the pair check the back window first which causes Esteban to move back before they turn their attention to the officers up front. Without a word, they nod their heads after making eye contact with the men. Backing away, they watch as two soldiers move their hands forward as the driver shifts his attention. Focusing on the open road ahead, the engine starts to rumble as they make their way through the shadows of the gate.

As the smell of burnt grounds fill the air, we look around the air catching the sight of patrols making their way back and forth. Back and forth, the men tip their heads as their guns remain to their side. Getting farther from the opening gate, the bar drops behind them as they continue deeper. Driving through in silence, the car turns and twists past various bunkers and hangers along the way. Watching as they continue without any idea of destination, the car starts to slow as another man approaches the car from the right side. Struggling to make out the words they were saying, I turn to Esteban sensing his helplessness from his reflection. After a couple of minutes, the man backs away and salutes before allowing them to drive by.

Once more the engine rumbles as exhaust spews out the back as the car rumbles forward as it heads toward a massive hanger. Ahead of us a mixture of darkness and faint lighting, we charge forward as we make the turn inside. Splitting the lines of troops, the man stops the car just feet from a pair of MiG-23 with their latches wide open.

Now this is where I knew that truly our lives had taken a turn from tranquil to chaos. For you see before our eyes, we watch as a pair of soldiers trolly out a large missile from out of a large metallic crate. Along the side of its metal plating, the Russian flag painted along one of the sides. Getting closer, we stare as they shut the door of the crate before putting their attention back on the trolley. Heading toward the car, they pushed it past us as we stare out the foggy window. Clearing the reflection, we watch as the stoic soldiers continue their trek out the door. With its flickering lights and bright wires, we watch as they turn the corner before disappearing. Before we can turn our heads, the front passenger door opens, allowing the man to step out. Once he was out of the car, one of the soldiers outside the car approaches the driver's side.

CHAPTER 5

Pulling on the handle, the man pops open the driver's door and steps around, giving the man a clear runaway to step out. Placing his boots on the floor, we watch as he steps out and takes a couple of steps before looking around. His nostrils flare as he continues his search around the room when suddenly his head stops. With a snap of his fingers, we watch as a man comes around the corner with a glass bottle in hand. Streaking to a stop, he hands the bottle to the man as he cowers with anticipation.

"Coronel Lins, hemos recibido noticias de que sus lideres se estan reuniendo," a voice says.

Nodding his head with a smirk, we watch as he stares at the swirling brown liquid within the glass. Then after gently coughing, he stares at the shiny cap keeping the fluid within the container. After taking a moment, he turns toward the man and shakes his head. Sensing the fear, he watches as Col. Lins turns his back to him as he makes his way toward the back of the vehicle. Approaching the trunk, he pulls open the leathery cloth and reaches inside as the man besides us drops his head.

"Que hay mal amigo?" I ask the man as he lifts his head up just a smidge.

"El machete de mi papa esta ahi," he replies softly as I turn back to the rear as I watch Col. Lins pull the machete out from a wrapped cloth. Waving it around, he momentarily makes eye contact with me and gives me an evil smirk. Before he can say a word, he turns back around as the covering closes behind him. Shifting our attention toward the side once more, we watch as he stands in his spot when he looks over at the man standing inches from him.

"La proxima vez abrelo por mi," Col. Lins commands before holding the bottle straight in front of him. Then as we all watch on, suddenly a banging sound rings out which shifts our attention. Looking back, we see a set of soldiers standing in front of the door when one reaches for the handle.

"Ven conmigo," the man yells as one by one we exit the car. Once we were all out and in line beside the Humvee, the sound of glass shattering turned our attention toward the other side. Before our eyes was just a taste of what was to come during our lifetime here, Col. Lins standing with a half-broken bottle in one hand and the machete in the neck of the soldier beside him. Watching with a smile as the man reaches for the wound even as blood gushes down, Col. Lins lets go of the machete as he admires the bottle. Clearing the glass from around the top, he smirks as he looks down at the floor seeing not a loss of a single drop. Then as he lifts the bottle to his mouth, the soldier beside him falls with a thud as the life within him fades away.

Chugging through the contents, he pulls the bottle away and slams it beside the fallen soldier before smiling as he looks down.

"Esa bebida es lo major que nos ha dado el enemigo," Col. Lins says as he looks at the swirling pile of blood and glass. Then as we continue to watch, Col. Lins kneels and then pulls the machete free as he sprays blood into the air. As he gets back to his feet, he looks at the weapon as droplets continues to drop from its blade. He then turns his focus toward a group of soldiers gathering up and points his fingers at the fallen soldier. With a nod from each one, they charge forward and pick up the man's corpse from off the ground. Before they can move out, Col. Lins places his hand up which causes them to stop in their place. He then lifts the shirt of one of the men and places the bloody machete along the side of it. Then with one foul swipe, he wipes the blood off the blade, leaving nothing more than a red smear. Once he watches the shirt slip from his grasp, he turns to Esteban and I before turning to the man besides us.

Without a word, the group of men takes the soldier's corpse away as Col. Lins throws the machete into the ground. Chipping some of the cement ground, the machete falls to the ground as it echoes off the sides of the hangar. As I watch the group disappear around the corner, my ears catch the sound of footsteps, which shifts my attention to Col. Lins. Seeing his approach, I take a tiny step back as I watch his expression change from stoic to a slight smirk. Before I can get any further back, I feel the gun of the guards behind me which shifts my attention to Esteban.

"Oh, valientes luchadoras, dejame darte la bienvenida a nuestras filas," Col. Lins says as he stops just short of us. Before any of us can turn at one another, he extends his hand out to us, starting with the sulking man all the way to the end.

I watch him gulp down some saliva before he cautiously lifts his head as he spots Col. Lins's hand sitting in the air. After a moment of hesitation, the man nervously extends his arm out to the colonel who reaches out and grabs hold. As the man's eyes spread open, he watches as he shakes his hand violently. After a couple of moments, Col. Lins releases his hold before shifting his open palm to the next man. After watching the same interaction happen to him, I prepare myself for my turn as I watch as Col. Lins shifts his attention toward him.

"Es un placer," I say out of the awkward silence for a reason still unbeknownst to me. Once the words slip out, I watch as his hand pulls back as if in disbelief that one of us spoke. I can even feel the stares from your dad onto my shoulder, wondering why I had said even a word.

"Como te llamas soldado?" Col. Lins asks as he reaches his hand out once more.

"Mario," I reply cautiously as I extend my hand out as well. Watching them connect in the center, he shakes my hand for a moment with a nod before he turns his attention to Esteban as he stands beside me. With his arms behind his back, I watch as Col. Lins reaches out for his hand. Keeping his arms stiff, Esteban looks down at the Col. Lins's hand when he starts to unlock his hands from behind his back.

"Coronel, sus invitados han llegado," a voice says, shifting the attention of all of us. Taking back his hand in haste, I watch as Col. Lins shifts his attention toward the opening in the hangar.

"Me dirigire alli ahora," Col. Lins replies before turning to us. Then after nodding his cap, he turns back toward the soldier and heads his way. Leaving us alone with the pair of guards at our back, my attention shifts to Esteban as he remains stoic.

"Ustedes cuatro vienen con nosotros," one of the guards says as he moves around us. Before any of us can think to escape, we watch as another group of guards approach from the opposite side. As all four of us nod are heads in silence, I watch as the two men make their way towards the front as they follow the guard. After a couple of seconds, I turn to Esteban to see him now with his hands to his side as his eyes start to dart around. Just as my lips prepare to speak a sentence, I feel a pointy object hit me in the square of my back a couple of times. Looking over my shoulder, I see another guard with the muzzle of his gun a centimeter from my shirt. Gulping down some confidence, I turn toward the other two men as they begin to make their way past the Humvee.

"Hurry up, comprende," the man yells as once more he jabs the gun into my back.

Feeling the anger start to build up, I clench my fists when I feel somebody grab my shoulder. I turn my attention to see Esteban with his hand firm on my shoulder with that stupid smile he has before turning his focus toward the others.

"Nosotros estaremos libres un dia," he says to me before starting to make his way toward the group. With his large steps, he rejoins them within seconds as I start to catch up with them. Furthering myself from the guards, I make my way to his side as I turn to Esteban to see the smirk still on his face.

"Tu siempre eres el fiel," I whisper to him as he nods his head just as we take our last step within the hanger. Once outside, the sun blinds us momentarily causing us to pause for a moment to allow our eyes to adjust. Continuing our patrol, we gather up into a tight circle and watch as we pass by groups of soldiers doing various activities. From preparing their guns to running laps around the base, they would turn toward us as we would pass them by. Hearing their whispers as we make our way, they would return to what they were doing once we were steps away. Seeing the men of various shades preparing themselves for whatever battle in ongoing, we continue as we finally stop just outside of a brown bunker with a large wooden door.

As we make our approach it has become increasingly clear that our lives are forever different. With each step on the creaking floorboards, Esteban and I made our approach behind the guard. Watching him reach out for the rusty door handle, he pulls it open, allowing us to see inside the barracks. From the forest green bunk beds to the bare mattresses, we walk inside as the guard remains in the doorway. The four of us start to look around at our new surroundings when we turn our attention to the guard as he starts to chuckle.

"Welcome home recruits," the man says as before we can reply he slams the door in our faces. With the door shut, we turn back to our barracks as laying in front of each mattress was a set of clothes. It was our military uniform as now we were no longer just farmers from the outskirts, instead we were soldiers. The biggest surprise is always you think it cannot affect you especially when you hear about it in the news from the safety of your farmhouse. Yet here we are, inside of a bunker with two other men who start to nonchalantly walk around. It was also especially hard on me as I had not been outside of my land in over a dozen years. Now, I stand in the center of this barrack before sitting down on the mattress where I can feel every spring coil up.

"Is there no escape from this place?" Esteban asks, breaking loose the awkward silence.

"Did you see any?" Mario asks back as we see Esteban shake his head.

With a deep exhale, I place my palms up against the metal frame and stand myself up. Shifting over to the smudgy window along the cement wall, I look out to see as the variety of activities continue to commence. From the moving airplanes to the dozens of patrolling guards, I continue to look around the base in search of an opening. That is when I see a drainage hole along the wall just big enough for us to escape out of and into the free world. Then just as I am about to turn my attention to tell the rest, suddenly there is a pounding on the door.

Stepping back to the rest of the group, the door erupts open to reveal Col. Lins with two guards flanking at his side.

Standing in silence, Col. Lins leans over to the pair to his left as they keep their rifles close to their chest. Continuing to watch, he points over to the two men beside me. Snarling his face, we watch as the two men walk up to them and pick up the clothes that sit beside their beds. Throwing them over their shoulders, the guards shove them into the sunlight beaming from the doorway. Once they were gone, Esteban and I turn to each other with a gulp before turning back to Col. Lins. Hearing a gentle cough, we turn our attention to him as he glares a hole through our bodies.

"Get your clothes," Col. Lins commands as we look over at the clothes beside our bunk bed.

Turning my attention, I watch Esteban walk over to the clothes and grab a seat before he turns to me. Throwing it at me, I catch them before placing them over my shoulder. Picking up his, he turns to me and makes his way toward the door. Gathering, we watch as the remaining guards wrap their hands around the clip and trigger when Col. Lins extends his hands in front of them.

"They have their clothes now take them to the locker room," Col. Lins says as he looks over at the guards who relax their hands. Backing away, Col. Lins nods as we start to make our way toward the opening.

"What is going to happen once we finish?" I ask as I watch Esteban make his way onto the staircase. Once my sentence was out, he stops and turns back before looking over at the Colonel. Turning my attention to the Colonel, I see him snarl before taking a step closer to me. Then as his hot breath fills my nostrils, I watch as he looks me up and down before stopping as he stares into my eyes. Then as he shifts his focus toward Esteban, I see him turn back to me with a grin. Continuing to wait for his reply, he reaches out and grabs the collar of my shirt before picking me up from the ground.

"It is up to you," Col. Lins replies finally as he releases my shirt which causes me to drop to the ground. As I fix my shirt, struggling to regain my breath, I gulp down some saliva before turning my attention back to Esteban. Seeing his hand motioning me forward, I lower my head before making my way toward him and the guard by his side. Approaching the Colonel as he stands his ground, our shoulders get close as I make my way toward the step. Then just as I feel the edge of the first step, hands shove me in the back, causing me to lose my balance as I stumble downward. Lucky enough, Esteban catches me before I eat dirt when I turn my attention to the top stair.

"Do we have a problem?" I yell as I hear the area of the base around me go silent. Looking around I see Esteban step back as Col. Lins smiles before taking a step closer to me.

"Do we?" Col. Lins replies as he looks around at the space with a grin. Turning my attention once more, I see the same soldiers who had gone quiet are now pointing the rifles in my direction. Their eyes focusing in, my anger forcefully subsides as I turn back to Col. Lins to find him down at ground level. He turns his head to the side and points out into the crowd when suddenly I watch as the group of camos around us splits open. Revealing a muscular man in tight camouflage pants, he steps out before cracking his knuckles.

"What is he going to do?" I ask as my eyes continue to switch between the soldier and Col. Lins.

"He is going to make you apologize," Col. Lins replies as he watches the man take a pair of thunderous steps. Except it was not toward me, instead it was toward Esteban who retreats. Before he can take another step, the soldier reaches out and grabs hold of Esteban's shirt tail and pulls him closer. Once he was within reach, the man turns him around before delivering a sucker punch to his left cheek. Spinning around as he stumbles to the ground, I watch as Esteban's hands brace themselves along the dirt when his face turns toward us. Blood dribbling from the crease in his lip, he spits out a glob of saliva before getting back to his feet.

Then with a primordial scream, Esteban delivers a return blow only for us to watch it barely faze the man. With a chuckle, he turns his face allowing us to see a red mark on his cheek when without notice he begins to wail on Esteban delivering a rapid series of punches. After about three or four, he grabs Esteban by the wrists, keeping them down to his side. By now, my anger has had enough as I prepare to charge into the melee. Before my feet can take a single step, I catch sight of a pair of soldiers holding me back. I then turn to Esteban only to watch the soldier hit him with a massive headbutt. Watching as my friend falls back first on the dirt, plumes fly up as Col. Lins makes his way between us.

"Tell him to stop," I yell as Col. Lins laughs as he watches Esteban struggling to regain his footing.

"Then accept your fate," Col. Lins replies as he holds his hand up, which causes the brutish soldier to stop any advancement.

Continuing to see Esteban struggle, I grit my teeth as I hold my tongue with all the self-control in my being even as my friend struggles to his feet. His hand up against his ribs as blood slides down his cheek, bouncing off the bruises that are beginning to form. Tears growing as you can sense the rise in his pain level, I turn to the proud soldier chuckling at the sight of Esteban's state.

"For the spirit of Cuba against all outsiders," Esteban yells as his hand releases the side of his ribcage. Now to most this is just an ordinary saying but to Esteban this was something he says when he tries to regain his strength. Personally, I have heard this only twice before and neither time ended well. Now yes, the odds were against him especially as I watch the group around us gather their rifles like dirty laundry. Of course, for those times, I will tell you later but just know that knowing this history causes me to break free from anger's grasp. My muscles relax as I watch him charge toward the brute. Wrapping his hands around his waist, he roars behind his bloody teeth as the man braces himself. Yet as helpless as I felt for the situation to my surprise I watch as the man's feet slide a bit in the sand.

"I accept," I say as I watch Col. Lins attention turn toward me as the brute shoves Esteban back a few feet. Suddenly, the crowd falls silent as the soldiers behind me release my arms.

"What did you say?" Col. Lins asks.

"Why did you say that?" Esteban asks as he spits out another blob of bloody saliva. Lowering my head, I try to avoid eye contact because I know that I was just trying to avoid further bloodshed and further injury to a man I consider a brother. Yet something causes me to look at my friend's face to catch sight of a mixture of anger and confusion the second we make eye contact.

"It's because he knows that he is weak," Col. Lins replies as I carefully pick my head up as I watch the rest of the group break apart. Continuing to bite my tongue, I watch as the muscular monster shoves his way through the group before disappearing into the base.

"Is this true?" Esteban asks as he momentarily shifts Col. Lins attention. Without a response, I drop my head once more which causes Col. Lins to turn his attention.

"Yes, and as punishment both of you shall clean up the barracks," Col. Lins replies with a chuckle before turning his attention to the open space left behind by the brute. Left in silence, Esteban and I stare at each other as the rest of the group separates. I walk over to him as his attention shifts to Col. Lins as he continues to walk away.

"Why did you stop me?" Esteban asks me as we watch Col. Lins make his way out into the distance.

"We are going to need our strength to get out of here," I reply as I struggle to search for an opportunity to escape. Yet the more I look and the more I search, I find nothing, not even the opening I thought I saw before. Oh, the thought of our crops being left dying in the boiling Caribbean sun. Yet before I can get any deeper into thought, two soldiers walk past us and toss shirts at us before chuckling as they walk away. Before either one of us can say a word, two airplanes take off, which set off the sirens around the base. Causing us to look around, we drop the clothes and charge toward the gathering group of people along the fence line. A row of ladders lock onto the platform as some of the soldiers begin to climb up.

Not thinking twice, we charge forward and make our way toward the back row of the gathering. Continuing to make our way through, we scoot past a few men who are trying to observe when we see a plume of smoke rise over the wall.

"I wonder what's going on," I say as I turn to Esteban.

"They are trying out some new bombs," another man says as I shift my attention toward him. Seeing him turn away from the group, I look back to see Esteban making his way up the ladder which forces me to follow behind him. Rung after rung, we climb ourselves to the platform as we stand side by side. Then just as we search the sky for the planes, we hear buzzing when suddenly a round of explosions lift from the ground. The planes fly off as our hands grab hold of the barrier as Esteban's eyes water.

"What is it?" I ask him as I take a step forward.

"That was our land," Esteban replies as his head drops in sadness. The fireball mushrooms upwards as the reds fade to gray. Once the glows fades, we look toward our family's property to see as the once luscious grounds were as brown as the sand along the beaches. Gone were the trees and buildings, as now all that remains is a singular massive crater. Our jaws drop as we try to find an ounce of normal hiding behind the ash and ember façade. Feeling the despair growing we lower our heads as our hands tighten their grip around the cement guardrail.

"That is just a taste of our new power," a voice says as coughing turns our attention. Looking back, we see the evil grin of Col. Lins as his shadow extends past the edge of the platform. Without another word, he lifts a glass and swirls around the last bits of the liquid that remains within. As I feel my lips open as I attempt to talk, I stop when I see his hand rise as he places the rim into his mouth as the brown, bubbly liquid slides down. Once it was completely empty, he looks back over the railing and launches the glass over the base wall.

"At what cost?" I ask, sending his attention back to me as his grin falls into a snarl.

"Nothing that matters," Col. Lins replies as he swiftly turns his attention back to the smoldering ruins. Still feeling the slight of the loss, I turn to Esteban who looks over his shoulder at the black smoke still rising from the crater where our land once stood. Then after seeing a pair of tears fall from his eyes and down his cheeks, he turns around with his hands in fists. Seeing his anger, I step between them to shield Col. Lins but more importantly to protect Esteban from any kind of retaliation. Screaming and grunting, I push him back as he huffs and puffs before I turn back to Col. Lins as I hear him start to laugh.

"What is so funny?" I ask, trying to calm down Esteban as he continues to stand aggressively.

"This is the first time I have seen any potential out of this one," Col. Lins replies as he takes a step closer.

"Oh yeah, why don't you come closer, and I'll show you even more," Esteban replies with a sneer. To my surprise, Col. Lins takes another step forward and stops alongside me as I try to protect Esteban from doing anything brash.

"How about you harness that anger and use it for the benefit of Cuba," Col. Lins replies as a slight bit of confusion hits as I can see Esteban's eyes shift in focus.

"Why would I help you?" Esteban asks.

"So, you and all your friends can get out and back to your lives," Col. Lins replies as he motions a hand out to all the men standing on the ground level. Stepping to the side, I watch as Esteban approaches the edge as he looks over at the men beneath as they remain silent. Then turning his attention to those around him still taking in the destruction, he watches as they nod their heads causing him to shift his attention back to Col. Lins

"I'll do it," Esteban replies as he turns his attention back to the ruins of our lands. These words shock me as I had never heard him speak more definitively in the time, I have known him. Yet there he stood as stoic as a statue, his hand flat alongside his thighs as he turned his attention back to him.

"Well then there is only one last bit of business before we move you," Col. Lins replies as he extends out his hand. Seeing his hand approach Esteban, I watch as he reaches his own outward as they connect in the center.

"What would that be?" Esteban asks as suddenly Col. Lins freezes the handshake.

"To remove your weak link," Col. Lins replies as with his other hand, he snaps his fingers. Suddenly, our eyes turn to the ladder as the vibrations from the climbing shake the floor. Once up on our level, I turn to Esteban who turns to me with uncertainty when I shift my attention back. Just as they arrive at the incoming soldiers, I watch as they attempt to grab hold of me when I start fighting for my freedom. Delivering punch after punch, two of them drop to their hands and knees when suddenly I feel the collar of my shirt lift into the sky. Higher and higher, I turn around to see Col. Lins holding me up like a baby kitten.

"What are you doing?" Esteban asks when he attempts to charge forward. Except before he can get any closer, two soldiers pull out their handguns and aim them in his direction, which freezes him. His hands lifting high, I watch helplessly as another set of guards charge forward and direct Esteban down the ladder. Once he was out of view, Col. Lins releases his hold, which causes me to recover my footing.

"Where are you taking him?" I ask angrily as I turn around. However, before I can take any action, the guards whom I had not been too kind to return vigorously. One grabs a hold of my arms as the other proceeds to club me in the back of the head. Feeling myself drop to my knees, I look up dizzily at Col. Lins as he takes a couple of steps forward.

"Don't worry about it," Col. Lins chuckles before delivering a punch which connects with my cheek.

Sending me spinning around, I fall flat on my stomach as my eyes struggle to hold their sight. Then just before I can lose all feeling, I watch as the guards gather around Esteban with their guns in hand. Making their way from me, I hear everything fall into silence except for the maniacal chuckling of Col. Lins as he remains behind me. Suddenly things go blurry as my eyes relinquish their grasp as darkness overtakes everything. Shortly after, the laughing stops and the sounds of my breathing fall faint as it becomes the sole sound I can hear. Even as I am barely holding onto consciousness my only thoughts are about where they are taking my friend. Yet this was merely a turning point as time would pass and finally, I came two days later in the medical tent with wires and tubes all around.

CHAPTER 6

Iwas not sure how I got there nor how much time had passed but I would get my answer as a military doctor came inside when I was taking in my surroundings. After explaining to me that days had come and gone since Esteban was taken and that I had lost a substantial amount of blood, my head dropped back onto an old potato sack underneath my head. As my eyes shut as the depression starts to grow, footsteps start to echo into the room. Catching my attention, I see a pair of figures making their way closer as I slowly recognize the man to the right. It was Col. Lins as my sight comes together when suddenly beside him a nurse walks in beside him. Before long, my eyes shift back to Col. Lins as I feel anger corrupt my mind once more as I continue to wonder where he had taken my friend. Watching as my hands tighten, I watch as Col. Lins motions to the nurse as she makes her way around me.

"You definitely took a spill," Col. Lins says as his lips lift to a tiny smile.

"Where is Esteban?" I yell as I start to attempt to get up from the bed. After a couple of seconds, I realized that there was a leather belt keeping down to the bed.

"Your friend is advancing through our ranks of the Cuban division," Col. Lins replies as he turns toward the nurse as I turn my attention as well. I watch her as she makes her way over to a silver tray with a cup of clear liquid and a brown napkin with a pair of tablets on top.

"Colonel, his next dose of pain relief is due," the nurse says as she rolls the tray over to my side. My eyes remain on her as they meet her brown eyes that sit beneath a mop of brown, flowing hair. Then after hearing another round of footsteps, I turn my attention away to see Col. Lins making his way over to the opposite side. Stopping beside my hand, he reaches down with both hands before grabbing hold of mine, beginning to pat the back of it. Then as I watch his expression sour, he strongly pats my hand repeatedly and then releases it as I look down at the red skin on top of my brown pigment.

"Thank you nurse Roxanne," Col. Lins replies as he smirks before turning his attention to the doorway. Making his way toward it, I turn toward the nurse as she puts the pills in my mouth. As I close my lips with them inside, she turns to the paper cup and brings it closer to me as I turn away from her.

"Don't worry it's water I brought it from the station," Roxanne says as I cautiously turn back.

As my eyes follow it into my mouth, she places the lip into my mouth and lifts it as it allows the cool liquid inside. As it puddles above my tongue, I swallow it down along with the pills as I keep eye contact with her. Feeling the peace of her smile, I rest my head back onto the makeshift pillow and close my eyes as I wait for the pills to take effect. After a couple of moments, the traces of pain fade away as I drift off into slumber. It was days later and various steps of progression afterward when I finally got out from the tent and the watchful eyes of the nursing staff. Days went by until I was finally put in a group with some of the weaker soldiers to help me get back into form.

Day after day, I went through the motions of my new life keeping my eyes out for your father. Yet no matter how many soldiers I see, not once did I ever see him. After 1 week, I had about given up hope of ever seeing him again when suddenly during a patrol I saw a sign. Making my way past the warehouse, I turn to the left and see Col. Lins when I heard his voice. I just knew it was him, so I stopped, which forced the rest of my group to continue. Between the anger for the Colonel and the concern for my friend, I hid behind some crates when I try to get a better look of him. He turns to the back of a plane nearby and motions his hand forward when suddenly I watch a soldier come forth. In front of him is a missile on top of a yellow metal cart. Taking a few steps forward, it starts to steam and spark as he continues toward the Colonel.

"Private Martinez, watch for the radiation on that warhead," Col. Lins says as the man stops before turning his attention to the Colonel.

"Yes, Colonel," the private replies before bowing his head. Before long he turns his attention back to the open gateway as I try to avoid any eye contact. As I duck behind the side, I watch as he makes his way toward the opening before turning his trek in the opposite direction. Keeping silent, I watch as he struggles to keep the warhead on the cart as it bounces with every bump. Leaving a stream of smoke and radiation in his wake, he continues forward in a zombie-like trance as I struggle to wonder what had happened to him.

"Mario are you okay?" a feminine voice asks, sending my eyes in the opposite direction. Seeing Roxanne approaching, I hear the cart come to a screeching stop which momentarily shifts my attention. See even before I shifted my focus, I knew exactly what this meant. Esteban stopped his cart and was looking at me except before he could take even a step, my attention shifts back to see Roxanne as she places her soft hand on top of my arm.

"Yes, I'm fine just trying to try and find an old friend," I reply before turning back to Esteban as I see his face. Yet instead of happiness or excitement, I feel sadness as before me was a man I did not recognize. Eyes and hair were a distinct color as the scars along his face controlled more than his brown skin. Sweat beading down toward his chin, he shakes his head when I hear a piercing whistle that almost blew out my ear drums. Once that fades away, the man turns back toward his cart and proceeds forward as he disappears around the corner.

"Any luck?" Roxanne asks calmly.

"Sadly, no," I reply as I turn my attention back to her.

"Well before you continue on, take this water I brought before you dehydrate in this Caribbean sun," Roxanne replies when suddenly I watch her turn back to the medical tent across from us. With a smile and a nod, I kindly take the water before taking a sip.

"Can someone get me a bottle of arsenic?" another voice chimes in which momentarily shifts our attention before he disappears behind the door. Hearing no answer, I take another sip before watching as she makes her way toward the clinic when she stops just shy of the opening. Then before she goes in, she turns her head towards me and smiles with a wave goodbye. Before I can reply, she fades into the darkness as I turn my attention back inside of the hangar. Looking inside, my attention immediately shifts to Col. Lins as he sits between a pair of soldiers as they stand on each side. Watching as his lips move about, he then points toward the nearby plane. Splitting from the Colonel, I watch as he gets up from the stool and then makes his way toward the opening. Then before he can get any further, a soldier sprints past me and stops just short of Col. Lins.

"Col. Lins, I have come on your recommendation," the soldier says as he bows his head and neck.

"Yes, tell me how Esteban has done in his advancement through the levels," Col. Lins replies as the man picks his head up.

"We currently have him securing the last of the warheads from out of the artillery," the man replies as Col. Lins nods his head.

Turning my attention to the base around me, I find myself on the opposite side of the artillery house. Taking the last sip of the water, I drop the bottle before making my way around the base. Progressing toward the artillery without interruption, I come up to the side of it to see a man squatting beside a warhead on top of a metal cart. Strapping the last part down, he wipes the sweat from his brow as it drips down onto the hot covering. As bits of steam erupt from the crevices, he stands back up and looks around before catching sight of my approaching shadow. Getting closer, the man starts to cower when suddenly the door to the unit bursts open. Sending him downward, I turn my attention to the open doorway to see another man in full army fatigue.

Resemblance uncanny, it hits me that this was none other than Esteban, your father. He was no longer the worrisome man going beyond his farm for the first time. Instead, he stands tall with laser focus on the young man beside the warheads. Continuing to watch the brewing interaction, I squat beside an oil barrel as I poke my head out a little bit.

"Sir Martinez, I have finished securing them down," the man says as he points at the individual carts. Turning to your father, he turns toward the young man before approaching the first cart that was closest to him. Reaching out for the first strap, he stops when suddenly he turns his attention to an approaching shadow. Looking over as well, I turn to see Col. Lins making his way with a man beside him in a lab coat. Now I pause and digress because at this moment it was ironic. The man beside Col. Lins is none other than the scientist that I had seen dead in the hallway. Yet at this point they stand side by side, approaching Esteban as the younger man continues to retreat another step.

"Nice to see you again Esteban," Col. Lins says as I watch Esteban salute the man. Angering me as I wonder what could have been done to force him to salute the man that beat me up. Struggling to hold it in, I watch his hand go down as he watches the scientist approach the warhead. Kneeling beside it as he inspects the strap, the scientist smiles, and nods before standing back up. Pulling a pen from his coat pocket, he jots down on a piece of paper on the clipboard before him.

"Everything check out?" Esteban asks as he and Col. Lins both look on.

"Indeed, which is good especially with the power one of these hold," the scientist replies as he looks up from the paper.

"Absolutely which is why we need to have that one specifically brought carefully," Col. Lins commands as he points to the one beside the artillery house.

"Why that one?" Esteban asks as he looks over at the warhead.

"That information is confidential," Col. Lins replies just before the scientist can open his mouth to speak. As the conversation drops, the young soldier cautiously turns around before darting out of the area. Now after a few moments of silence a horn sounds off from the opposing side of the base which cause Col. Lins to turn to Esteban.

"What is it commander?" Esteban asks.

"Bring that to the hanger immediately," Col. Lins replies as he points to the cart inches from him.

"Yes sir," Esteban replies as he places both hands on the cart.

"Be careful, that is an important experiment," the scientist replies as he watches Esteban beginning to make his way toward the hangar.

CHAPTER 7

While I was busy eavesdropping, I forgot that in his trek for his destination stands the oil barrel that is hiding me. So, before he can get any closer, I duck back just before he can get a glimpse of me. Holding my breath to keep quiet, I hear his footsteps pass by as he continues his journey. Then as I turn around another round of explosions rang out from another drill test. After feeling nothing, the ground starts to tremble and quake as I struggle to brace myself against the barrel as I can hear the liquid swish back and forth. Feeling it lessened, I turn my attention to Esteban to see him struggle to maintain balance when shockwaves fade away.

Continuing further, he makes his way down the open path when suddenly one of the straps on the cart comes free. To his horror, the straps swing up before flopping to the ground beneath one of the back wheels. Instantly he stops but not before the strap gets caught on the wheel, sending the warhead bouncing on the cart. I then watch as Esteban looks back at the artillery house to see neither Col. Lins nor the scientist to be there.

"That was close," Esteban whispers as he kneels beside the cart and grabs hold of the wheel. Lifting it up, he pulls the strap free before getting back to his feet. However, as I watch him grab the end of the strap, my attention turns to see a spurt of radiation shoot out from a crevice on the opposite side. Turning my attention to the area around us, I see not a soul in sight as I turn back to Esteban. Then as I watch in silence, he starts to pull the strap tighter before bringing it down to the ground. However, just as he is about to close it up, the air horn at the base goes off, when suddenly I see a large plume of smoke appear beyond the wall.

Feeling nothing at first, the ground starts to shake as the alarm silences. Looking at Esteban, I watch him unsteadily fall over as he releases the strap, which bounces around the shifting soil. Then just as the ground calms, the warhead continues to bounce and move on top of the cart until suddenly it rolls toward the edge. Slamming into the bar that prevents it from hitting the floor, a loud clang echo outward. Holding our breaths, Esteban stands still as a siren like the air horn starts to go off as the lights on the panel along the warhead start to light up. Flashing and blinking, Esteban looks at the control panel and starts to press different buttons to no avail until finally the alarm silences.

Exhaling, Esteban steps back when out of nowhere the buttons all turn red and the screen above reads ARMED. His eyes widening in fear, he starts to look all over for any aid when he spots me behind the barrel. Trying to avoid eye contact I looked away even as I felt his stare piercing a hole through my neck.

"Officer, come here quickly," I heard him say which causes me to cautiously look down.

"Yes sir," I reply as I turn my attention back to him. Before I can step out completely, the word on the screen changes to RELEASE as suddenly all the other lights along the panel turn black. Seconds later, the panel pops forward and releases an explosion of light which launches Esteban into the wall as I struggle to keep my hands over my eyes. Between the ringing in my ears and the blinding light, I struggle to gather my bearings when my knees encounter the sandy ground. Then as sudden as the explosion came it dissipated allowing me to stand back up as my eyes adjust. Examining the scene, I see Esteban motionless along the floor as the warhead remains on the cart. Stumbling forward, I look over at the panel along the side to see it blank as I turn my attention back to my fallen friend.

Listening to the subsiding ringing, I kneel beside him to see the moving dust in front of his lips. From the blast his body sits in shreds of fabric from his clothing. Scrapes and scratches up and down his arms and face, blood slides down his skin as it piles up along the grains. Yet something caught my eye as through the splitting skin cells glowing liquid centipedes its way into his body. As my eyes follow the liquid from his body, I watch as it heads through the sand and toward the cart.

"See now you see why I never left my farmland," I whisper as suddenly I see his eyes slowly open. The more they did, the more the liquid dissipated into the Caribbean sun. Once his eyes are open, he struggles to get into a sitting position as he braces his hands around chunks of sand.

"Mario, is that you?" Esteban asks faintly as he struggles to keep himself upright. However, before I can answer, stampeding footsteps ring out which causes me to shift my attention in their direction. I watch as Col. Lins and company come running down the path and then toward us. That is when I had to decide about what to do as I deliberate whether to leave my friend or not. Turning my attention to him as he regains his strength, suddenly time freezes when my eyes watch as his muscles swell, and his wounds heal.

"It is me old friend, are you ok?" I reply as we watch as the last few scratches fade away.

"I think so," he replies as he looks down at his hands, beginning to flex them into fists.

Now it was the oddest thing I had seen at the time yet after a few more seconds, he was completely fine. He then turns to me with a blazing fire in his eyes as I back away when my eyes catch sight of him lifting off the ground. Then as our eyes see the approaching Colonel, he drops back down to the sand as his familiar brown eyes return.

"Get away from him," Col. Lins yells as after a few more feet he stops at Esteban's side. Doing so, I back away toward the dented oil barrel as I try to hide my face from them.

"What happened?" Esteban asks as I look back to him as we momentarily make eye contact. I then watch as Col. Lins kneels beside him as the scientist that I had seen before makes his way over to the broken panel along the side of the warhead.

"It appears you had an accident," the scientist says, sitting the panel on top of the cart before turning toward him.

"Is it salvageable?" Col. Lins asks.

"Yes, fortunately for everyone here the nuclear canister within only sprung a tiny leak," the scientist replies as he reaches inside the opening and pulls out a metallic cylinder. Showing Col. Lins, the item, he points out the hole inside before placing it into his lab coat pocket. Once it was away, he momentarily shifts his focus onto Esteban as he continues to look down at his hands. Seeing this, Col. Lins looks over at Esteban as well to see the same thing.

"Are you able to continue?" Col. Lins asks, standing up from the ground. As they look at Esteban whom remains silent, they watch as he turns toward them. Placing his hands back along the side of him, he gets up as well and turns toward the two men before drifting over to me as I continue to stand beside the oil barrel. Before Col. Lins can look over, he turns back to stare at them before making his way over to the cart.

"Of course, not even a scratch," Esteban replies as he makes his way around to the steering handle. As his hands wrap around the metal bar, it indents from the force of his new strength. Feeling the change of surface, Esteban's eyes widen in surprise as he sees the power of his grip. Shifting his eyes around the room, he struggles to avoid contact with them before wrapping his fingers around the bottom of the handle. Then with little hesitation he starts to push it as the wheels start to move.

"What are you doing?" Col. Lins asks as he steps in front of the cart.

"Bringing it to the hangar," Esteban replies.

"Are you forgetting something?" the scientist asks, pointing down toward the loose strap that is still sitting atop the warhead. Esteban smirks before looking down at his hands when I can see some sweat bead up. Soon his face reddens as an orange glow starts to overtake his throat when suddenly I did something I should have done sooner. Before any action can be taken, I swiftly make my way past the Colonel and the scientist before kneeling beside the warhead. Feeling their stares, I grab the strap and place it around the mechanism as I lock it into place. Once secure, I stand back up as I look over at Esteban as the orange glow starts to fade.

"All secure for transport," I say aloud as I turn to face Col. Lins. Seeing his half smile, he folds his arms as he nods his head.

"Thank you," Esteban replies, breaking the silence.

"Well, it is nice to see you supporting the cause," Col. Lins says as he shifts his focus to Esteban. Without saying a word, Esteban grips the handle once more, bending it further when he starts making his way toward the storage hold. Getting further, my eyes follow him as he turns the corner when I start to hear footsteps closer to me. Turning myself as I feel a hand grab hold of my shoulder, I see Col. Lins smiling as he stares through my soul.

"How can I help you, Colonel?" I ask, saluting him as he releases his grasp.

"You can start by making sure that he makes it to the storage safely," Col. Lins replies.

"Will do sir," I answer before hastily walking in the direction of where I had seen Esteban. Hearing not a word to break my stride, I continued forth before cutting the corner before seeing Esteban deliver one final shove to the cart. As above the night had begun to settle, the glimmer of the metal around the rolling rims starts to make their way into the storage. I found myself suddenly walking faster as I saw Esteban stumble toward the ground. Watching my walk turn into a run, I see him fall flat to the ground as a plume of dirt and sand lift into the air.

It was at that moment that the simple life for him ended for as I got to his side, the man I knew was not who I had seen before me. His body had an orangish glow as his muscles started to spasm and swell. I watched helplessly as he started to convulse as his eyes and hair started to change colors. Groaning in pain, I tried to pull him beside the cart only to struggle mightily as if he weighed as much as a dozen boulders. Yet there he remained on the floor as I watched his eyes shut and his body freeze. Helpless as I continued to watch on, I mourned as I saw the color on his legs and arms weaken along with his fading breath. Ceasing altogether, I rushed to his side where I grabbed his arm only to watch his pulse continue to fade. As his lips sealed up the remnants of his last breath, I looked all around the campsite with tears rolling down my cheeks.

Helpless as I find myself alone, I looked back at my friend as above us the dark clouds return. Even throughout the misery and sadness, I knew one thing about Esteban was that he would not want to be at peace in this chaos. Beyond the walls of the base and the craters from the falling bombs, the remnants of our homes remained. That is when my eyes started to search for an exit when a pair of Humvees entered the base from about three barracks down. Suddenly, my attention shifted to a spare cart sitting alongside an alley. Rushing over I grabbed hold of the handles before I turned it back toward my fallen friend as he remained motionless on the ground. Stopping alongside his body, I kneeled beside him as I placed my hand on his chest. Feeling each slow heartbeat, I drop a half dozen tears along his fatigue jacket before I wiped the rest away.

"I'm going to get you out of here my friend," I whispered as I gulped down some strength. As I dug my hands and arms beneath his body, I started to attempt to lift him up from the sandy ground. Then after a pair of failures, I clenched my teeth as with one final extension of my strength I managed to pick him up. Hastily laying him down on the cart, I took off my own jacket before I laid it across his body. As I made sure to cover his face with the lower part, I looked up toward the exit as the rain started to fall. Then with a deep breath, I started to wander toward the escape as I made sure his body remains uncovered.

"Where do you think you are going with that body?" a voice said, causing me to turn my attention. Seeing another officer with his gun still in its holster, I struggled to come up with a proper response.

"I am going to bring it to the graveyard," I replied as I watched the soldier make his way over to Esteban's body. Before I can speak another line, I watched as he reached down for the jacket and pulled it down to see his still face.

"Do you know how he died?" the soldier asked as he left the shirt in a bundle around the neck.

"He was found in his barracks like this," I replied as I started to reach down for the fold of the jacket. I then turned to the soldier before I shifted my focus to Esteban, and leaned over before the soldier launched a glob of spit on his chest. Angrily, I pull my arm back as I resisted the urge to attack when suddenly the soldier takes a step back before he pointed toward the exit.

"Change of plans directly from Col. Lins this man is to go to the water beyond the sugarcane field," the soldier commanded as I replied with a nod.

"May I ask why?" I asked.

"This man has chosen to escape his dedication to his country so he shall join the other traitors in the sea," the soldier replied as another approached us from another direction. Turning his attention, I began to grab hold of the cart when I see the man drop to a kneel.

"Randolf, what is going on here?" the man asked as Randolf lowered his head.

"I have instructed this soldier to bring this corpse to the open sea to be removed from your camp," Randolf replied before he stepped toward the side. Turning our attention to Col. Lins, we watched as he approached Esteban's body before stopping at his side. Shaking his head, he covers his face back up with the jacket before he turned back to me.

"Only thing more shameful than a soldier who refuses to a fight is one who betrays his country," Col. Lins said as he turned to Randolf.

"Do you agree, soldier?" Randolf asked as he and Col. Lins both turned toward me. Realizing the potential direness of any answer, I nodded my head in approval as I tried to avoid their eye contact.

"Well, then soldier please dispose of him with no honor," Randolf replied as I nod my head once more. Turning my attention, I saw out of the corner of my eye Randolf making his way over to Col. Lins. As I made my way toward the exit, I stopped for a moment to look back. Seeing them head in the opposite direction, my breath eased as I continued forward before I made a left toward the last guard post. Going forward as my eyes directed themselves around to the other side, I see the guard standing watch on his patrol.

"Good day," I said randomly as I continued past him.

"Where do you think you are heading?" the guard asked as I froze in my tracks.

"To the sugarcane field to dispose of this body," I replied as I pointed down at Esteban. Turning to the guard, I saw him nod even as he made his way closer to me.

"Col. Lins has instructed me to guide you there safely," the guard replied as he stood at my side.

"Safe from what?" I asked.

"Mines, ambushes, and crocodiles," the guard replied as he pointed out toward a shriveled section of grass.

"Well then come on then," I said back as I continued my trek toward a clear section of mud. After a few more steps, the first row of sugarcane came into view as we continued to get closer. Once we arrived in silence, we stopped ourselves between two rows when suddenly a plane blasts overhead. As its exhaust cleared the space, clouds bundled up as rain started to fall. Growing angrier by the second, the weather started to deteriorate as I looked over as the man turned his attention toward me.

"Let's get this over with," the guard said as he walked around to Esteban's feet. Wrapping his arms around his dirty military boots, he lifted them from the cart as I approached Esteban's arms. Once he was in our possession, we made our way through the rows of cane until we started to see the shifting water of the Caribbean. After we passed the final pair, we lowered Esteban down to the ground when I watched the guard turn around and find a pair of shovels. Tossing one to me, he turned to me before he made his way to a section of dirt beyond the reach of the tide. As his feet touched the moist sand, he started to shovel up some of the ground before he stopped to look up at me.

"What is it?" I asked.

"Get over here and help me," the guard commanded.

"Or what?" I asked. Before even speaking a word, he slammed the shovel into the ground and reached down to his side. After he unsheathed the top of the holder, he pulled on the handle as it revealed a metallic blade with a layer of dry blood.

"Get over here," the guard yelled as the rain started to intensify. Swiping at the large drops that landed on his face, he wiped them away as I made my way forward. Beginning to shovel the dirt, we watched as the size of the hole expanded as the dirt under our feet puddled up. Then after throwing back one last shovelful, we both exhaled before we turned our attention to Esteban's body before the guard focused in on me.

"Get the body," the guard commanded as he slammed the shovel into the muddy ground. Bundling my fist, I gritted my teeth before I turned my attention to Esteban's body as his arm draped over the edge of the cart. Exhaling deeply, I charged over to the cart and attempted to lift the body with some strain. Feeling my muscles tighten, I felt him lift from the cart before I turned around back to the guard. Carefully, I made my way toward him before I gently placed his body down beside the hole. Before I could attempt to slide him in, the guard pushed me out of the way and knocked him inside. As he landed with a thud, his body settled into the mud as I turned my attention back to the guard.

"What next?" I asked, watching as he pulled the shovel out before he loaded up a first load of mud.

"Hide him from the allies," the guard replied before he threw it down upon Esteban's body. As some of it slid down his chest, the jacket crumpled under the weight as it pressed up against Esteban's chest. Revealing the cold, blank expression on his face, I watched with angst as the guard lobbed another chunk of soil on top of him. Then before I could make a move, the clouds started to twist as the rain continued to intensify. Lightning and thunder started shortly which sent my eyes upward. Hidden behind the shadow of the night, the swarming rainfall increased as suddenly the water beside the farm grows choppy. As the wind swiftly picked up from all directions, the guard looked around as he delivered another shovelful onto his body. As it covered him up, the guard slammed down another as the sugar cane started to bend as it swayed back and forth.

CHAPTER 8

Once the final bits of skin was hidden away, the guard threw down the shovel onto Esteban's body. The second it landed, lightning crackled through the sky at the same time as the rising waters beside us started to climb and then slid down over the edge of the hole. Breaking the barrier, the downpour continued as a pair of lightning strikes landed around us. Then just as the thunder could rumble, his walkie talkie buzzed through the flurry of wind gusts. After a couple of seconds, he fumbled about before bringing it toward his face.

"Lt. Alvarez is the deed done?" the voice said before it dropped out.

"The body is buried Col. Lins," Lt. Alvarez replied as he looked down at the ground where we put the body.

"Ok now get rid of the other," Col. Lins's voice rang back as I watched the guard shift his attention back to the walkie talkie.

"As you command," Lt. Alvarez replied before he placed the walkie talkie back along his belt loop. Once it was secured, he turned his attention to me as his hand slid down the other side. As he pulled up the folds of his shirt, he pulled out his machete from its sleeve. With it high into the air, his eyes glazed over as he struggled to maintain his balance on the puddled ground.

"What are you doing?" I asked as I lifted my hands up.

"Colonel's orders," Lt. Alvarez replied before he shoved me to the ground. When I tripped over the lip of the hole, I slipped as I crashed into some of the sugarcane on my way to the ground. Cushioning my fall, I grimaced momentarily before I watched as his footsteps got closer to me. I then turned my attention; I saw the blade as it swayed in the air even as my hands fumbled around the muddy ground. Just as I saw his evil smirk, my hands wrapped around a stalk of sugarcane as I tightened my grasp. Then just as he attempted to take a swing, I go first as it hit him across the side of his face. Momentarily stunned he gathered himself when I pushed him backward which caused him to trip over the same lip that gotten me. With him down, he started to use the machete as a crutch even as I attempted to get up as well.

As he angrily swiped at the shifting waters, he turned around as he tightened his grasp. Letting out a scream, he charged at me when suddenly he stopped as a loud roar vibrated the ground. Suddenly the water from the Caribbean pulled back as the rain above started to weaken to a drizzle. Meanwhile, the puddle of mud along the ground started to bubble as steam started to lift into the air. Drying out the soil over the hole, the ground started to crack and vibrate as we continued to retreat from the site. From the openings, embers rose from the ground, and spurted out of one end as our eyes looked on in shock. Then before either of us could move, we watched as a forearm rose from the section of dirt as a hand tried to escape from the tomb.

"Don't move," Lt. Alvarez yelled as he once more attempted to lift his machete into the air. Before he could get it into the air, another lightning bolt slams down into the hand which knocked both of us backward. Coming to a crashing halt, we slammed into the ground as I started to lift back to my feet. Turning my attention, I watched as the cloud of dust and dirt fell when suddenly a pillar of flames rose from the dirt. Mixing with the moisture in the air, parts turned to steam as embers continued to head toward the clouds.

"This is exactly why I don't venture outside of my farm," I said as I carefully headed toward the opening. Before long, the flames vanished as I started to see a shadowy figure as it examined its hands as steam released from its entire frame. Then before I could get any closer, the figure's eyes lifted upwards which allowed me to see a pair of circular flames. Dodging through various stalks of bent sugarcane, I continued forward as the flames faded before I got within feet it. Then as I stepped forward, the figure turned to me as I stepped into the light to get a better look. Suddenly it hits me as the light of the moon broke through a pair of clouds. Before me, Esteban stepped out from the dirt grave as he took another step further away.

"Esteban?" I asked, watching as the figure shifted its attention toward me.

"Yes, what are we doing here?" Esteban replied as he looked down at his hands before he turned back at me.

"You died," I replied as I stepped closer to him feeling a pair of tears streak down my cheek.

"Wait, the last thing I remember is the steam from the warhead hitting me," Esteban said as he continued to look around at the surroundings. Before I could speak, a series of gunshots and explosions rang out beside us which sent us down to the ground. Feeling the musty dirt in front of my mouth, smoke started to surround us before I turned my attention over to Esteban. Shockingly he was not there as I covered my head when another round of shots sounded off. Then before I could keep my head down any longer, someone grabbed me up when suddenly I started to hear a whistling sound. Our eyes look upwards when we saw a plane pass by as a bomb falls a mile or so away. Fear and sadness took over, I turned to Esteban as I watched his eyes shift over to the deep opening in the ground from where he rose back to the surface.

"Sorry but this is going to hurt," Esteban said as before I replied he shoved me down inside. Down with a thud, I looked around as he momentarily appeared over the lip of the hole.

"What about you?" I asked as he instantly turned to look back at me.

"I have the flaming passion of a Cuban storm," Esteban replied as his eyes burned inside out with flames. His skin glowed as steam rose from his pores, he turned toward the location of the bomb when a loud explosion erupted. The sky lit up with hundreds of orangish shades that take the night sky back to sunset. Before long, one burst of winds followed which sends Esteban's feet toward the lip until he took another step forward.

Curiously, I climbed my way back to the surface as my fingers tried to attach themselves to the shreds of muddy dirt beneath them. Then with a strain, I pushed myself upward when I saw Esteban in front of a wave of flames and smoke as the eruption expanded for miles. Silently saying about a dozen prayers, I watched as he stood there with his arms to the side. Then as the wave continued forward, Esteban stepped forward as the last few bits of his military uniform burned to ash as flames rose through his skeleton.

"I believe in you, brother," I screamed as he turned back for a moment to show the smirk before he turned back. I then dropped down to the bottom and sat along the side of the hole. With my hands above my hair, I shut my eyes as for a moment the darkness brought upon a peace and silence. However before long, the bright glow of the approaching flames forced my eyes open as I felt the heat as it suffocated the space around me.

Then as the immense heat got closer, Esteban turned back and unleashed a channel of flames from his mouth which split the explosion in half. Creating a moat of air between the two sections, he started to spray the flames left to right to create a barrier. Taking away the oxygen from the area, the flames extinguished as the rows of sugar cane turned to ash. With nothing but broken lands in its wake, things fell silent as the flames turned to embers. Cindered ash left all around, I looked all around as my ears continued to hear nothing beyond my faint breath. As I prepared myself mentally to make a move, the sounds of footsteps coming closer sent my eyes back to the opening.

"Come on up," Esteban's voice said as he reached his hand toward me.

Smirking as I looked at his ashy hands, I grabbed hold as with ease he pulled me back to the surface. Once there, the devastation momentarily took over me as I felt tears start to well up. My eyes then make way to the first row of sugarcane that once stood feet from me. I then made my approach when I reached for a half-burnt leaf as it turned to shambles within my grasp. As the ash fell from between my fingers, I looked back at Esteban as he stared deeply into his hands.

"What happened to you?" I asked as he shifted his attention.

"I have no idea," he replied as a round of gun shots echoed about.

"We need to go back to the base," I said as I started to head toward the large walls a few miles away. When I turned to him, he nodded back as he started to walk beside me as we made our way toward the outpost. With each round of steps, we made our way through the burned remains of the farm before we arrived uneventfully at the road. Coming to a stop, we turned our attention to one way to see flames as they rose into plumes of fading smoke. Meanwhile in the opposite direction, we turned to the base as we saw spotlights which spun throughout so you heard the faint sounds of engines as they roared within.

Undoubtedly this was truly symbolic, for the fight going around us matches the one deep within both of us. For you see, the island of palm trees and heart is being devolved into chaos and turmoil. War throughout has taken hold as gone are the days when the only smoke was from tobacco cigars. Now we must choose to return to a place where we know not what to expect over a military base where our enemies remain in force. With a gulp and a sigh, we turned our attention toward the base that sits just a few miles away before beginning our trek toward it. Step after step, we got closer as each moment we got further away from the simple life we once knew. Our simple paradise, our home gone in a blaze of exploding ammunition as we maintained our focus in front of us.

As we approached the guard post with little opposition, we passed as I stared into its chambers seeing no sign of Lt. Alvarez awaiting our arrival. Getting deeper into the base, we made our way between the rows of housing as night continued to control the sky.

"Can we stop for a moment?" Esteban asked as before I could turn my head, I heard a thud. When I turned around, he started to struggle to get himself back up to his hands and knees as I rushed to his aid. With my arm placed around his back, I boosted him upward when suddenly his limbs started to give.

"What did that warhead do to you?" I asked as my friend started to shiver and shake.

"I don't know," he replied weakly as suddenly all his weight crumbled down to the ground. As I struggled to get him back to his feet, I managed to roll him over to his back. I then watched as his skin struggled to maintain its natural pigmentation as oranges and reds started to rise into his ribcage. Then as I saw his mouth open agape,

I spotted flames as they swirled within. Then just before any more flames could rise, I stumbled back a couple of steps as the silence from around started to suffocate us.

The calm is broken swiftly when I nearly hit a pair of barrels as I watched Esteban release a stream of flames from his mouth. As I struggled to avoid the bright light from the fire, I turned away for a moment as I started to smell the ash as I watched the embers drop around me. I then dodged out of the way in time to see the fireball as it lifted just above the top of the wall. When it made its way over, it burned the particles in the air as they fell flat to the ground. I then watched as the strength of the heat lessened which allowed the air to return to normal. Once normalcy is brought back to the area, I look down the pathway to see not a trace of another but especially no Col. Lins.

My attention returned to Esteban when I saw his body no longer there as I searched all around for him. Finally, I saw him back on his feet as his face sat hidden behind his arms as they leaned against the wall of the storage shed. From there I knew especially when he angrily punched the wall which shifted the entire unit over an inch or two that things could not be the same. Somehow or someway that chemical release from the warhead has forever changed my friend. The days and nights afterward, I watched over him as I tried to keep his emotions in check as we learned more about his newfound powers. One by one we learned more about his abilities such as his increased strength, fire breath, and the craziest of all is flying. Yes, flying like the heroes in comics and in movies one in the same.

One minute he was flat on the ground like us and the next minute his body was flying among the floating clouds. Overall, I would say we did an excellent job hiding his powers until one day he had no choice but to reveal them to everyone on the base. The worst part was because of my recklessness that he had no choice. Now, when I fast forward, I want you to realize that at all points of this fight, Col. Lins is always creeping in the background with his spies.

About a week or two pasts of us training unbeknownst to the others and yet Esteban continued to struggle to harness this new strength. I sat along the top stair as I watched an approaching thunderstorm coming from the south as I can feel his angst of him as he tried to hover. After he tried every comical pose, he squatted just above the sandy ground as he stared through the grains beneath his feet. As the first set of tears slid down his cheek and hit the floor, rain started to fall from the clouds. With the drops that crashed about, lightning started to crack in the distance when I started to see watch as he struggled to keep his composure.

"Be free my brother," I said as I looked down as I meet with his bloodshot eyes as another round of tears started to flow.

"How can I?" he muttered back through the crying.

"The sky is your freedom," I told him as I lifted a finger up toward the trembling skies. I then watched as his eyes followed my finger upward as he started to stand back up. As my attention turned to him, the emotions calmed like the ocean on a windless day. His silent confidence became admirable as he exhaled deeply with eyes shut before he spread his chest. With his hands out to the side, they erupted open when suddenly the grains of sand around him started to levitate. Seconds later, his feet lifted from the ground as my eyes started to rise along with him. Then it happened, I watched him in awe as he lifted higher into the sky like the towers that I had seen on the television.

With a roar, he took off into the chaotic skies as I watched his shadow shrink to a dot. Prideful, I lowered my eyes as I placed my arms to rest on my knees. As droplets began to fall on my skin, I heard a loud scream which forced me to turn my attention to a tent just down the street. Just as I leaned forward on the stairs, another scream caused me to jump up and take off toward the sound. Going tent by tent, I sensed no distress until finally I heard it again coming from the colonel's barracks just beside the airplane hangar. To no surprise, the base fell silent as a pair of guards made their patrol under the metal roof. Then as I am about to turn back in the other direction, I heard another scream as this time a door erupted open.

When I turned my attention, I am in shock when I see a women dragged from out of a tent by a muscular guard. Getting closer, I watched as she started to fumble a vial about from hand to hand. Then to my surprise I found it to be none other than Roxanne the nurse as she passes through an area of moonlight between a pair of clouds.

"Help me, someone!" Roxanne screamed as she tried to pull her arm away from him.

"Did you really think you could get away with taking samples of arsenic?" a voice replied from inside the tent.

"I didn't think it was important," Roxanne said as she tried to free herself from the man's grasp.

I then watched as he pushed her into the street until she stumbled to the ground. Suddenly, glass shattered all over the sand as she struggled to get back to her feet as another man stepped out. As he took off his lab coat, he threw it back inside before he turned his attention back to her.

"I'm going to bring you to the Colonel so you can be punished," the man replied.

"Please somebody help," Roxanne yelled as the man snatched her arm and started to drag her down the street. Then after I watched them take a couple of steps, I knew I had to do something, so I jumped into the light. The man stopped on my appearance as momentarily he released his hold before he chuckled in my direction. Then with a crack of his knuckles, I continued to seize up the muscular guard when suddenly my memory started to kick in. This man before me was none other than the one that threw me down the platform and into the medical tent.

"You will pay for this!" I yelled as I took off my shirt to show the strips of bandages as they covered my torso.

"Let me finish this," the muscular beast roared as he charged forward as the man watches on. Coming toward me with a barbaric rage in his eyes, I braced myself for what was to come when a strange energy charged through me. Before I could defend myself, he delivered a combo of blows which sent me to the ground. That is when I heard Roxanne's screams, so I turned to look as I struggled to ignore the pain encompassing my body. Then as I went to speak, the man grabbed hold of my neck and picked me up to my feet before he delivered a knee to my sternum. The next thing I know is I feel the taste of iron along my lips which caused me to slide my palm up against them. Pulling it forward, I saw the red blood along my brown skin which made me look over to Roxanne as tears started to flow down her cheeks.

"You're coming with me," the man said as he approached her as once more, he grabbed her by the arm. With his hand around her wrist, he started to drag her away when something inside told me I needed to fight back. So, the next thing I know my hands ball up into fists as my muscles swelled and tightened. Now, this is the part where the hero makes a comeback as I started to swing for the fences. When that first blow connected, it sent the man for a loop as I unloaded another set of strikes. One after the other landed flush with the man's face and chest. As he stumbled around the grounds, I looked down at my bloody knuckles as a calming came over me that I had not felt since I was picking bananas from my land. That is when my attention shifts to the man as he began to pull Roxanne down the road.

"Somebody help me!" Roxanne screamed as she tried to flail around as she almost dislocated her shoulder.

"No one is left to help you," the man replied as a faint rumble of thunder echoed about. As he continued forth, the man charged ahead as she let out a scream when I started to take a step toward them. After having forgot about the other man, I prepared to take another step when suddenly I heard a roar from behind me. Before I could turn around, the man speared me and sent me face first into the ground. Unable to get free from his massive frame, he pushed himself upward using the center of my back when he started to rip off some of the webs of bandages along my skin. Going after it like a wild beast, he then started to deliver a series of punches to my back before finally he got back to his feet. Unable to get to my own, he laughed as he made his way over to my head. He then placed his hand on my head like a coconut from a palm when he pulled me up as sand rained down. As the rain continued to pour down, he forced me to watch Roxanne as she is taken further away.

"You are never going to see her again," he said when he released his hold which sent my face back down to the ground.

As I squinted to avoid the grains, my eyes caught sight of a plastic bottle with a mix of sand and water building within. After I watched the man come closer, I secretly grabbed hold of it as I watched him make his way in front of my face. Then without a word, he lifted his military issued boot over my head as he prepared to deliver the final strike. "Say Goodbye!"

Then before another breath could be had, he paused as a reddish glow covered the base as it allowed me a moment of opportunity.

"Not tonight," I yelled which shifted the man's attention. Before he could slam his foot down, I rolled away before I got back to my feet. As he shook the pain from his boot, he then charged at me as I hid the bottle behind my bruised back. When the glow dimmed above, I waited until he got within striking distance to take my chance. That is when I struck, I brought the bottle forth and squeezed it with all my might which launched the mixture of sand and water into his face. Causing a distraction, I threw the bottle to the side as he attempted to clean off the sand. Before long, I charged forward as my muscles swelled once more as I made my approach. Just as he emptied the area around his eyes, I made eye contact with him which stopped me in my tracks.

My hips twisted as my arm pulled back when I unleashed a blow onto his face which caused him to lose his balance. As I watched him struggle to keep up, I turned to him before I brought both my hands down onto the back of his head. He collapsed to the ground when I stepped back as I watched him lay motionless along the sandy floor. His chest and back still, I made my way over to the bottle that I threw aside. Once it was in my possession, I stood back up and placed it into a canteen that sat along the back of the man's belt. As I started to unhinge it, I heard a faint groan as grains of sand blew from in front of the man's mouth. I then shook my hand at the sky before turning my attention back to the man.

CHAPTER 9

Seeing a bright red stream split the dark gray clouds, I saw it spin around the air above the base as it dodged the falling rain. I knew well that it was Esteban as he continued to discover his own powers, I then turned my attention to see the man as he held Roxanne in front of another figure. As the clouds shifted about, the moon shifted its light to reveal Col. Lins as he stood in front of them.

"This is the traitor that stole our supply of arsenic," the man said as he angrily threw her arm down to the ground.

"I didn't do it," Roxanne wailed as she tried to hide her face from the glare of Col. Lins. After she heard nothing but silence, she looked up to see his frowning face as he folded his arms together.

"Stand up, women," Col. Lins commanded as we watched Roxanne as she rose from the ground. After she had gathered herself along the cushiony surface, she brushed off the dirt that remains when she continued to look between both Col. Lins and the man to her side. Without a word, Col. Lins turned to the man with a sneer before he walked up to him.

"What are you going to do to her?" the man asked as his haze bounced Roxanne and Col. Lins.

"What proof do you have Captain Randolf? Col. Lins replied with an angrier tone. He then watched as the man started to look around as the rain started to lessen around them.

"I have always been suspicious over these water bottles that she is always caring around," Randolf said as he looked over at Roxanne who lowered her head.

Col. Lins nodded his head in response as he turned to Roxanne as she slowly lifted her own to make eye contact with him.

"What shall your punishment be?" Col. Lins mumbled as he flexed his hands into a fist.

"Col. Lins, pardon my intrusion," I yelled out as I approached the area.

"Come forth soldier and speak to the lord of the base," Col. Lins replied to me as I continued to make my way forward.

I then stopped on the opposite side of the others when I saw Randolf turn to me before he looked back over to Col. Lins.

"Thank you, sir," I replied as I reached back for the canteen. As they tried to catch an early glimpse of the item, I pulled it forward as I watched them as they attempted to identify what I had brought out. Then before another word could be spoken, I tossed it to Col. Lins who momentarily fumbled it before he secured it within his grasp. I then watched as he looked at it before he turned his attention back up to me.

"A canteen?" Col. Lins asked as I watched as everyone's attention shifted to the item.

"Open it," I replied confidently as I maintained eye contact before I watched him shift his focus to the canteen.

As Col. Lins held the bottom, he grabbed hold of the top and spun it off as it flopped down to the sandy ground. I could then tell the moment he discovered the bottle within when his eyes widened as large as they could get.

"What is it?" Randolf asked as he struggled to get a glimpse of what is inside.

Meanwhile to my right, I saw Roxanne as she looked back at me in confusion when she turned her attention to Col. Lins who had the same expression.

"It's a bottle," Col. Lins replied as he tilted the canteen over as the bottle slid out from its depths. Instantly, Roxanne's eyes widened in shock before she tried to check her emotions. I then saw her turn to Randolf as his anger intensified.

"That's my bottle!" Randolf yelled as we watched Col. Lins as he dropped the canteen on the floor before he turned his attention to the bottle. As the liquid swirled inside, Col. Lins shrugged as he then turned it upside down before he placed back upright once the last drops were on the floor.

"Where did you find that?" Roxanne whispered to me. Without a response, I looked back at the fallen soldier who remained still on the sand. As she watched me turn, she turned as well before she momentarily glanced back at Col. Lins. Then before anyone could have said anything further, he tossed it back to Randolf who caught it carefully. After he brought it closer to his frame, he looked at it as the drops settled just above the thin layer of sand.

"What is so special about this water bottle?" Col. Lins asked.

"It's where I held my sample of arsenic," Randolf answered as he looked at the bottle once again.

"That is where I gave my patients water from," Roxanne said as she broke the monotony of their conversation.

"Well, it appears that it now has sand in it," Col. Lins chuckled as he pointed at the bottle.

"Wait, you gave this to patients; did they not think anything of it?"

Randolf asked.

"No, they just thought it went bad from the sun," Roxanne replied.

"Well as long as no one died," Col. Lins said as I watched Roxanne turn to me as I realized she had given me water.

When I placed my hand to my mouth, my mind started to wander at the thoughts of what arsenic can do ran through my brain. Then before I could get any further, the rain started to intensify which causes Col. Lins to retreat into his camp.

"May we enter sir?" Randolf asked as the rain crashed down around us.

"Yes, so we can discuss punishments for her theft and your carelessness," Col. Lins commanded as the two of them started to make their way inside.

"What about me sir?" I asked as I watched as their attention shifted to me.

"You have done enough here soldier," Col. Lins replied before he turned his back before he headed deeper into the main room. Without a response, I watched Randolf as he followed him as Roxanne lowered her head before she headed out of the rain. Then once they were all inside, I turned back toward the opposite end of camp where to my surprise I no longer found the soldier's body in the center of the road. As I figured he was taken by the medics, I took a couple of steps when suddenly I heard a crack of lightning from above. Before I could take another step, I heard a barrel fall over as I felt as something rolled into my boot. After I caught sight of it, I spotted a red apple along the chestnut brown ground as I kneeled to pick it up. Once it was in my grasp, I felt it give a little before I stood back up.

I then looked over to where the barrel fell when I heard a blood curdling roar. As my attention shifted, I watched as the bleeding soldier charged at me. Before I moved, his arms wrapped around my waist as he slammed me into the ground as I felt the air exit my lungs. As the apple jumped free, I struggled to break his hold when he shoved me deeper into the sand as he attempted to deliver a pair of blows. As the first missed, he started to rain down elbows into my sternum as it left a trail of bloody prints along my shirt. As each one got stronger, I attempted to defend myself when he delivered a punch across my cheek.

"You shall pay for your actions," the man yelled as he delivered another blow onto my other cheek as my head whipped in the opposite direction.

As beads of blood dripped over my eye, I caught a glimpse of the apple once more as the lightning struck which caused me to see the blending of blood along the skin of the apple. Then just before I could have grabbed it as an attempt of protection, the door to the house opened as the man turned his attention to see Col. Lins who just stood in the dimly lit doorway.

"What is going on here?" Col. Lins asked as for a moment the fighting ceased.

After he could turn his attention to me, I grabbed the apple as I hid it beneath my chest when I saw Col. Lins as he kept his focus on the man.

"Revenge," the man replied as I attempted to get up. Then just as I was about to push myself up to my feet, he then kicked me back over as I could see the streams of moonlight when they reflected off his face. When I saw the streaks of his crimson mask, I watched as he slid his hand across the right side of his face as it gathered up the blood. Then as he goes to ball it up into a fist, I watched as some of the blood slip from between the cracks in his fingers.

"Finish this and remember snitches are not looked kindly at this camp," Col. Lins replied as I turned my attention back to the man who pulled his fist back.

With that, I felt my strength renewed even as my hand tightened around the apple as I watched as the man's fist as he took aim at my face. Upon impact, I felt the pain bolt through my body as I could hear Col. Lins's chuckle between thunderclaps. Mocked as even the clouds applauded with their rumbles, I watched as this time the man lifted his boot into the ar. As chunks of sand fell from the indentations of his boot bottom, he attempted to deliver a blow when I managed to roll out of the way. With apples in hand, I pushed them down as I forcefully rose to my feet as I stumbled momentarily before I caught my balance. Feeling the cold of the blood as it dripped onto my skin, I turned my attention to the apple still in my hand.

"You're loca, but a dead man," the man chuckled before he attempted to charge once more. As he dove forward, I gritted my teeth as I slammed the apple into the side of his face. Watching as its juice and chunks flown about, the man fell to the ground as I saw an indentation along the side of his cheek.

"What was that?" Col. Lins asked as his eyes widen.

"Un Manzana," I replied as I dropped the core on the man's back as he groaned in pain from between the grains of sand. My head shook as I looked over at the broken shards of the barrel when I saw another beside it. I then kicked him on my way over to it before I picked it up with ease when I heard the apples inside move around. As I turned my attention back to the man, I lifted it to the highest my arm could go before I stopped myself, so his head remained between them. Then as I shifted my attention to Col. Lins, I slammed down the barrel onto his head as apples erupted in all directions. With nothing but the taps of the rainfall, my ears caught the sound of the man's breath being taken as suddenly I heard clapping coming from the doorway.

"You are really a loca manzana," Col. Lins said as he made his way back out into the weakened rain.

I then felt my feet back away from him as I watched as he stopped at the man's side before he nudged his foot up against the man's ribcage. He then knelt beside him and placed his fingers up against his neck.

"What have you done?" a voice asked, which caused me to look around to the doorway to see Randolf standing there.

"Loca Manzana here is taking this brute's place," Col. Lins replied as he stood up before he reached into his gun holster. As he pulled out a silver revolver, he aimed at the man to my surprise and shot him in the head as the bang echoed through the camp. As the man convulsed down into the sand, blood pooled up as it started to connect with the puddles of water that had grown from the daytime rain. He then placed the gun back into its holster before he nodded in approval toward Randolf whose jaw remained agape from the doorway. Then when he realized we were both looking at him, his emotions changed to his usual serious demeanor.

"Come with us to the Candy shop so we can get you ready for the coming war," Col. Lins said before he let out a tiny cough. Before I could reply, he stepped over the man's dead body and made his way toward the doorway as I saw Randolf step to the side. Once inside, I turned momentarily to the fallen soldier before my focus shifted to Randolf in the doorway.

"Now wait what about Roxanne and her theft," Randolf added.

"You are always about the group," Col. Lins replied as he continued toward the back door. He then turned to Roxanne as she sat in the corner atop a green and brown chair.

"What about your punishment?" I asked as I shifted my attention to him as his eyes started to dart around the room. When his eyes settled back down on her, he charged over and grabbed her arm before he pulled her toward the center of the room.

"Her crime was far worse as it could have endangered your life," Randolf replied as he stared at Col. Lins. As we watched as Col. Lins stopped at the back door of his tent, he turned to the three of us as I deliberated what to say. Then as I saw him nod his head, I watched as he stepped closer as once more, he reached for the revolver at his side. However just before he could get it out, the rain stopped as smoke streamed down from the sky just outside the front door. The man's body burned along with the sand, steam rose from the ground as it intensified with each second that passed. As we retreated, a shadow appeared along with an orangish red glow when suddenly from nowhere, Esteban reappeared with his feet flat against the crystalized ground.

"Who are you?" Randolf asked as he took another step back as I watched Col. Lins come closer.

My attention shifted back to Esteban as he stood firmly on the ground, I watched as the reddish glow started to fade. As the last bits dissipated from his eyes, he looked over at me with a smile before his sight shifted to the others in the room.

"I have been looking all around the camp for you," Esteban said as he pointed over to Col. Lins.

"I don't think we have met," Col. Lins replied as he examined Esteban as he looked around the room.

"My name is Esteban Morales and you have taken my life from me," Esteban replied as once more fire started to burn within his eyes. Then just as the flames rose from his sternum could be unleashed, gunshots rang, and everyone dove out of the way. As everyone cowers, I turned my attention to Esteban when I found nothing more than a vacant doorway.

"You will never catch me," Col. Lins chuckled before he opened the door only to find Esteban as he waited for him. After he took a pair of steps back, they both came toward the center as I saw Roxanne headed toward me as I hid behind a chair.

"He is all yours," Randolf spit out as he attempted to avoid eye contact after he made his way toward the open door. Coming within a foot of Esteban, he about made it through when suddenly I watched as he grabbed Randolf's arm and jerked him back. As he landed back down, Randolf broke free only to see his wrist being held by Esteban. With fire in his eyes, Esteban twisted it as he continued to try and get away.

"Come on Loca Manzana, attack him," Col. Lins yelled as he pointed over at Esteban.

I looked over at him with a smirk before I shook my head as Col. Lins charged at me in anger. Before he could get further, I watched him fall on his face as he then turned to Roxanne in time to see her pull her leg back. He then got up angrily and turned the gun on her. After he paused for a second, he placed the gun back on his side before he made his way towards me. As I tumbled over the bookcase beside me, he pushed me aside as he headed toward the door.

"Are you such a coward?" Esteban roared as Col. Lins froze his hand wrapped around the doorframe.

"I fight on my time," Col. Lins replied as he turned his attention toward the door. However, before he could make his way out, I placed my hand on his shoulder. Holding him still, he turned at me angrily as I shook my head before he turned his attention to Esteban.

"Your fight is with him," Randolf said as it shifted Esteban's focus to him as Col. Lins made his way closer. For a moment, Esteban relented as he released Randolf's arm as I watched him start to slink away. He then turned to Col. Lins with a nod as suddenly Col. Lins bolted toward the back door. As he stepped away, Esteban prepared to unleash a pair of blows when Randolf sucker punched him, stunning him momentarily. After it sent him back a step, Col. Lins charged toward the dock behind the base as Randolf attempted to follow him. Just as he got a couple of steps outside, he stopped in his tracks as Esteban launched through the roof of the building sending debris everywhere. After he avoided the sections of roofing, we watched as he reappeared outside between Randolf and Col. Lins.

Once more, Randolf attempted to deliver a punch except this time Esteban grabbed his fist before he twisted it at the wrist. Unable to break his grasp, he started to bash at Esteban's arm to get free only to feel his hold tighten.

"If you release me, I can tell you everything about their experiments," Randolf screamed as Col. Lins froze steps away from the yacht. With his feet pressed along the wooden pier, he turned back to see Esteban unrelenting at the pressure.

"Why would we care about that?" Esteban replied as he tightened his grip, the pain grew as Randolf even stopped moving to avoid further damage.

"I can bring with me the scientists who brought these powers out," Randolf cried as for a moment Esteban, and I looked on in curiosity.

"Ok then, tell me their names," Esteban yelled back as he weakened his grip momentarily.

As he felt the weakness in his grip, Randolf attempted to deliver a blow with his free hand as it brushed up against the side of Esteban's face.

Esteban then smirked when suddenly he unleashed an uppercut to his elbow as a loud snap echoed out as cries followed behind it. As Randolf screamed and groaned, tears rolled down his cheeks as he looked over at his broken arm before he turned to Esteban.

"Tell me their names now," Esteban roared in his face as for a moment I held an ounce of pity as his arm bruised. Then before Randolf spoke a word, a loud bang echoed out as a bullet struck just above his ear. Killing Randolph, blood started to flow downwards as the shock forced Esteban to release his hold. His arm limped downward, Randolf's knees gave out as he tumbled into the sea waters below. As his body disappeared beneath the depths, we shifted our attention back to see Col. Lins as he made his way toward the boat. Before we could take a step after him, gunfire rang out which shifted our attention.

CHAPTER 10

Only moments later we watched Col. Lins as he got to the boat as the engine rumbled. However, before any of us could make a move, explosions rocked various sites in the base as a pair of shadows zoomed overhead. Flames started to spread from building to building when we heard the screams of soldiers as they fall silent as more gunfire rang about. Then as we are about to turn our attention to Col. Lins, his barracks erupted into flames when we heard Roxanne scream from inside. I then turned my head to Esteban as he looked back at me.

"I got to help her," I told him as he turned his head as we watched as the yacht started to take off. Getting further, he turned to me and nodded before we both charged inside to see the situation. Through the doorway as embers erupted from the framework, we brushed through the smoke when we saw Roxanne as she cowered in the corner. As the flames continued to spread thanks to the wooden furniture that laid throughout, I struggled to figure out a plan to rescue her. Esteban then watched me as I zigzag through the obstacle course of furniture before I arrived at Roxanne. Her brown skin covered in ash, I grabbed her and carried her toward the open doorway. Having gotten feet from the entrance, beams of lights shot through as we froze just on the edge of freedom.

Then as we attempted to take another step, the sources appeared as soldiers' step inside before they pointed their guns in our direction. Our hands went up as the men grabbed us by the shoulders and brought us outside in front of a group of similarly dressed soldiers. With the garb of the Cuban army, they watched as I looked back for Esteban to no avail. My head shook for a moment when I turned to see the group of men circled us as they took one step forward.

"My name is Rodrigo, and we need to get you out of here," the man said as he approached me with rifle in hand.

"What about the gun fire?" Roxanne asked as I waited for their response.

"That was us," Rodrigo replied as the men around them lifted their guns into the air with a cheer.

"Ok but what the two planes?" I asked as they suddenly stopped cheering. They started to look at one another as even Rodrigo looked lost.

"They must have escaped," Rodrigo replied as the rest nodded their heads as the flames crackled around us.

"Are there more survivors?" I asked as I looked around the base as I watched bodies lay sporadically around the roads.

"Just you two," Rodrigo replied as it sent my attention back to him.

"Why do you think we aren't going to fight back?" I asked when suddenly the roof of Col. Lins's barracks caved in which sent embers upward.

"You aren't armed," Rodrigo answered before he pointed down at the empty gun holster along my belt.

"True, so what is the next step of the plan?" I asked as it lifted his eyes back upward.

"First, we give you a gun for protection and then we get out of here," Rodrigo replied before he turned to the man beside him. Seconds later, the man stepped toward us before he aimed at me. After he placed his rifle flat in his palms, he extended them out to me to allow me to take it. With the gun secured in my grasp, Rodrigo turned and charged toward the direction opposite of where the hangar now burned. One by one, we watched as the group charged with their guns at their side. Once the final one headed away from us, Roxanne and I looked back with no trace of Esteban anywhere in the vicinity.

"Hopefully, he got away," Roxanne said as I turned my attention back to her.

"Yes, now we need to make our own way," I replied as she nodded before we turned our attention toward the clear path. Then before any more time could pass, we made our way toward the others as we started to approach a massive hole along the side of the base wall. As we watched groups of parked Humvees just beyond the base, the men loaded up as Roxanne and I aimed for the one in the back. As I got there first, I opened the door to allow her in as I followed behind. After we struggled to sit comfortably in the back, we turned to the other side to see the door opposite open wide.

Watching as the two men ignored it, I turned to see a man in a black coat slide inside as he wiped the ash from his body. The man then shut the door as he placed his head back as we attempted to see his face past the hood. Then as he turned as we looked at him, the man momentarily turned to us just before the lights inside turned off. To my amazement it was none other than Esteban as the only thing that remained was the fire that smoldered in his eyes as he placed his finger in front of his lips. As we kept quiet, we nodded our heads as we watched as the darkness grew, he himself started to fade into it. We then watched as all that remained was the fire in his eyes, we watched as he turned toward the men in front as the Humvee started to move.

"Now that is where we get here to our current situation," Mario says as he looks over at Rafael.

"So, wait what happened to Col. Lins?" Rafael asks as he watches Mario shift his attention. Looking around the room, he wanders about before settling once again on Rafael.

"Your dad found his yacht months later washed up along an island off the coast," Mario replies as he looks over at the gray window.

"Si, para sacarlos de mi camino," a voice echoes into the conversation which shifts their attention toward the main doorway. That is when they see Col. Lins standing in the entrance as his outline darkens the hallway behind him.

"Bueno, sabiamos que las ratas siempre regresan a casa," Mario replies as he stands up from the ground.

Pressing his hands up against the bars, Rafael meanwhile gets to his feet as he remains dead center. Keeping his eyes on Col. Lins, they watch as he makes his way forward into the room. Behind him a set of guards approach from outside as they stand along both sides of him. As Mario watches as they shift their focus onto Rafael, Col. Lins meanwhile keeps his focus on Mario. Starting to make his approach, Rafael angrily looks at Col. Lins who approaches the cage bars before stopping just shy. Then as he tilts his head to gaze into Mario's eyes, he smiles as he reaches his hand beneath his jacket which sits overtop his tropical shirt.

"Loca Manzana, no puedes esconderte de mi," Col. Lins says with a smile as he pulls out a reddish apple from out of his pocket. Shaking it back and forth, he then begins to clang it against the bars before starting to chuckle.

Mario then angrily throws a punch when his fist collides with the bars, which bends them as Col. Lins steps back continuing to laugh hysterically. Mario then watches as he looks over at the guards as they keep their hands on the strap keeping their guns along their chest. Without notice, he tosses the apple over to the men who grab it before taking a bite out of it. With juice dripping down his mouth, he throws the apple off into the darkness as Col. Lins turns back to Mario.

"No te preocupes, solo estamos aquí por el niño," Col. Lins says as he points to the door of Rafael's cell. Watching as the guards' approach, Rafael steps back toward the wall as they barge into his cage.

"Where are you taking me?" Rafael asks as he struggles to get free as the two men grab hold of his arms. With his arms out of his control, they lead him forward and out the door. Squirming and shaking, Rafael continues to struggle even as they stop him at Col. Lin's side.

"Don't worry, your dad is joining us soon," Col. Lins replies with a smirk as he turns his attention back to Rafael. Quieting him for a moment, Rafael turns to Mario as he remains up against the cage door with his hands squeezing the surface of the bars.

"Solo dejalo ir tu calmo esta con nosotros," Mario yells as Col. Lins once more shifts his attention toward him even as Rafael turns his gaze onto Col. Lins.

"Tengo que tener un plan de respaldo," Col. Lins replies before turning his focus onto Rafael.

"Wait a second, you told me my dad was dead," Rafael screams as he starts to shake and squirm once more.

"I lied, now take him to the main room," Col. Lins replies. Once the last word is out in the open it causes the guards to grip harder as they watch Col. Lins point out the doorway. Shifting his stance as they direct him toward the hallway, Rafael looks to the side of Mario with a frown. Then with a nudge, they start to motion him out as they leave the two men alone. As their footprints fade from their ears, the two men look at each other as Col. Lins starts to smirk.

"Sabes que va a venir por ti, especialmente después de que mataste a su esposa," Mario says as he turns his back to Col. Lins. Remaining in silence, he walks over to the window and looks out into the rainy night as flames tower all around.

"Cuento con eso para poder matar a su hijo también," Col. Lins replies, which causes Mario to turn back around. Taking a step forward, Mario sees the toothy grin of Col. Lins as he stands on the verge of laughter. Before Mario can speak another word, Col. Lins turns his back as he starts to make his way toward the door.

"Por qué lo odias tanto?" Mario asks which causes Col. Lins to stop in the doorway of the hallway.

"Me quito todo y tiene que pagar," Col. Lins replies as he looks over at Mario who takes a couple of steps toward the door.

"Tu vas a pagar," Mario yells as he slams his fists into the door. Saying nothing as he turns his attention back to the hallway, Col. Lins takes another step before stopping once more.

"Nosotros veremos," Col. Lins says as he looks back momentarily.

"Puedes apostar tu vida a que lo haras," Mario replies angrily as Col. Lins continues to look as he lets out a snicker. Before he can say another set of words, Col. Lins starts to laugh as he places the top of his head up against the wooden doorframe. Then after stopping, he turns back to see Mario as he remains just on the other side of the cage door.

"Casi lo olvido antes de irme, dile a Roxanne que dilgo hola," Col. Lins says as he starts to laugh before taking a second to cough. Bringing his hand to his mouth, he continues to make his way forward as the door shuts behind him.

Leaving him alone with his anger, Mario turns his back to the doorway as the footsteps silence. Hearing nothing more than the rain falling against the side of the building, he approaches the window as the level of condensation grows along the surface. On his way, he cleans off the fog when he sees that sitting on the other end of the glass are metal bars like those of his own cage. Once the sight clears, he looks around at the chaos below the storm clouds brewing above. As lightning flickers through the sky, he backs away before looking down at his hands as he can feel his muscles start to spasm.

"¿Tormenta Cubano, donde esta tu?" Mario whispers as his eyes shut before tears can reach down to his cheeks.

As Mario dwells in his prison above him on the roof of the building, Esteban remains flat on his back. Rain steaming as it touches his body, his breath continues to strengthen as energy continues to channel through his chest. Seconds pass as he remains still even with the color of his skin beginning to return. Then as the clouds split from the moon, a pair of raindrops strike him on his eyelid as they steam on impact. Suddenly they start to flutter before rupturing open as they reveal their eyes before flames start to swirl into the center of their pupils. His mouth splits as a breath makes its way down into his lungs as he starts to regain motion in his limbs.

"Donde estoy?" Esteban asks as his eyes look down at the darts that remain in his sternum. Tilting his head to the side, he pulls them out each one stinging momentarily. Once they are out, he throws them off the building before making his way back to his feet. As the rain continues to bounce off, he stands back up before crouching down behind the ledge of the roof. Seeing the burning fires along with patrols of troops throughout, he turns to the guard posts as their spotlights shift around. Realizing he was out of sight, he turned around to take inventory of the area. Around him beyond the gravel and rows of sand, one building stands in the center of it. With a single viewing window in the center of the door, lights flicker inside as shadows move back and forth.

After trying to think of another plan, Esteban makes his way toward it when he notices the light fading to slivers as shadows leap from beneath the bottom of the doors. Preparing for the worst, he ducks into the darkness along the side of the building just in time to see the door burst open. From out of the opening, two men with guns at their sides step onto the rooftop before making their way toward the guard rail.

"Te criaste en un Granero?" another voice says which turns the attention of the others. Shifting Esteban's attention, he watches as one of the guards makes his way out before shutting the door behind him.

"Todos estabamos," another guard replies as the door closes shut. As the light dims with its closing, the moon above shines on the three men standing in a circle. Remaining still, Esteban's fiery stares as one of them reaches into his pocket before the others begin to do the same. One after one, they pull out a brown cigar from their pockets as one of them pulls out a matchbox. As each grab hold of a match, they strike it up into a flame as the reflection of the fire bounces off Esteban's eyes. Placing it against their cigars, the ends start to glow as they place it into their mouth. Then after their cheeks sink in, they release as they lower their cigar before releasing a trail of smoke.

"No deberiamos estar atentos a la Tormenta Cubano?" one of the guards asks as he lowers his cigar. Watching as the others look at each other before turning their attention back to him. Then as they are about to reply, they start to laugh as one of them takes another puff of his cigar.

"Me preocuparia que el Col. Lins encontrara con estos," the guard replies before taking another puff of his own. As the other guard looks back with hesitation, he smirks before taking a brief puff of his own. As he lowers his, one of the guards lowers his cigar before turning to the two men around him.

"Alguien sabe por qué el Col. Lins siempre tiene que tomar una bebida marron?" the man asks as the two shrug their shoulders.

"Supongo que es una adiccion como estas," the man replies before taking another deep puff of his cigar. As the three start to chuckle at the man's response, Esteban continues to watch as the men approach the guard rail of the roof. Watching on, the men release out the smoke within their lungs as it swirls through the air. Heading upward into the air, the smoke dissipates just shy of the cloud as the reddish glow from the flames abound suffocates the darkness. Even as the moon and its lunar silence glow, the sounds of gunfire and engines rumble about the base. Then, just as Esteban starts to move, series of explosions ring out in the depths of the Caribbean to the roar of the soldiers. As the lights expand into the shade, Esteban retreats as he heads deeper into the darkness.

Then after watching the men unload a few rounds into the dark sky, Esteban steps forward as the light starts to dissipate.

"Viva Cuba," Esteban mutters quietly as the flames in the depths of his irises return to power. As the glow lifts through his sternum, he approaches the men as the light completely diminishes. Returning into the darkness, the men take another puff of their cigars as the embers at the end brighten once more. Then as the men take another puff of their cigars, behind them a shadow approaches as red eyes open over their shadows. Suddenly the men turn around to see nothing before turning back with a shrug of their shoulders. Once their attention shifts, the set of eyes return when another eruption of flames reveal Esteban as his eyes bounce between the two men nearby.

CHAPTER 11

Then just as the light dwindles, Esteban reaches out to the two men nearby before grasping their shoulders. Surprising them, they attempt to turn back only to find themselves shoved over the top of the guard rail. With a scream, he watches as the two fly over the rail and fall rapidly toward the ground. Before they can land, Esteban turns to the last one who starts to shake and shiver.

"Tormenta Cubano no puedes ser tu," the guard screams before turning his gun on Esteban. Continuing to retreat, the man fearfully starts to fire off rounds as they fly off in all directions.

Chuckling at the cowering soldier, Esteban continues his approach as the flames start to inferno inside of his corneas. After the clip empties, the guard throws the gun at Esteban who watches it hit him in the chest before falling to the ground. Shaking his head, Esteban sees the man's eyes widen in fear as he starts to look for an escape.

"Donde esta Col. Lins? Esteban roars as he watches the man collide with the side of the building that once hid him from the guards.

"No se," the guard yells as he looks over his shoulder, seeing the predicament that lay before him. Gulping down some saliva, the man shuts his eyes before turning around to take a swing. Landing flat against Esteban's cheek, the man watches as Esteban turns for a moment before spitting out some blood. The guard then smirks as he looks at his hand as he sees not a trace of blood along his knuckles. Then before Esteban can turn, once more the man attempts another shot except this time Esteban wraps his hand around the man's fist.

"Te voy a dar una ultima oportunidad," Estaban says as he twists the man's arm until they both hear a loud pop.

Feeling a jolt of pain, the man screams as he tries to break Esteban's grasp by attempting to beat down on his thick fingers.

"No puedes hacar esto eres el héroe de Cuba," the man cries out as he drops to his knees. Suddenly, the flames in his eyes extinguish along with the glow in his throat. He then releases his hold on the man's arm, allowing him to bring it closer to his body as he tries to hide any kind of grimace. Then before he can say anything further, Esteban turns around and takes a couple of steps before freezing still.

"Lo lamento," Esteban mutters as he closes his eyes as a trail of tears starts downward to his sharp jawline.

"Lo que le paso?" the man asks as he struggles to stand back up. Keeping his arms in front of his chest, the guard starts to look around for an escape when he sees the entrance back into the building. The light shining behind it, the man starts to cautiously make his way toward it even as he keeps his eyes on Esteban who continues to stand with his back to him.

"Tanta rabia y venganza," Esteban replies as he wipes off the last few remnants of tears before taking another step away from the man. Continuing to get further, Esteban stares out into the collision of peace and chaos that is the horizon around the base.

Meanwhile, the man starts to shimmy toward the door as his hand wraps around the doorhandle. Then as his muscles strain, the door starts to budge as the light starts to escape from the cracks around the frame. Creaking as it separates from the structure, the guard turns back as he continues to see Esteban face the other direction. Feeling some relief, he starts to open the door faster until finally it reaches its apex. Once it was open, the guard once more turns back to Esteban who takes another step away. As lightning chains away from the base, the guard turns his attention back into the blinding light beyond the doorway.

"Una ultima cosa Tormenta Cubana," the guard says as he looks to see Esteban look over his shoulder.

"Hablar," Esteban replies as he continues to look back.

"Nunca escaparas," the guard replies, causing Esteban to turn his entire body around. Face to face with the man, he sees a patrol of guards in the doorway that dim the light. With their guns taking aim, the men start to place their fingers on the trigger as the guard between them makes his way toward the other men.

"Un momento," Esteban replies as he looks down to find a dimming cigar as it sits helpless along the cold cement. Freezing the guard, he turns back to see Esteban kneeling as he places the cigar into his grasp. Then with it between two fingers, he stands up before looking at the last few embers. As the flame in his eyes start to match, he looks at the man who stares back in confusion.

"Ultimas palabras antes de morir," the guard says as the sounds of the men placing bullets in the chamber start to ring out.

"Ninguno listo para ver como las cosas se convierte en humo," Esteban replies with a smirk. He then starts to place the cigar into his mouth when smoke starts to stream outward. Then once the connection is made, the fading embers start to brighten in intensity as the orangish glow rises from the depths of his sternum. As his eyes shift back to the men, fear starts to rise in their souls as the guard turns to the others.

"Disparale," the guard screams. Before another word can be spoken, gunfire starts to ring out as it forces the man to dodge out of the way. Watching on, the bullets make their way toward a smirking Esteban as the smoke continues to lift into the air. Suddenly, the glow starts to radiate from his neck and cheeks as Esteban drops the cigar back to his side. Then just as the bullets can get any closer, he unleashes a blazing flame toward the group, incinerating the bullets on its way.

Their eyes widening in fear, the men scream as they turn to run only to watch as the flames make their approach. Swallowing up the doorway as the lucky couple of men make it down the stairs, the explosion rattles the structure down to its core.

As flames and smoke fill up the stairwell, the two men wipe the ash from their faces as they start to search for any survivors. Finding no trace beyond piles of ash, the two look upon each other in horror before turning back at the gray fog as it settles into space. One of the men approaches the stairs when suddenly from out of the smoke a projectile pops free from the smoke. Watching as it bounces along the floor before coming to a stop just inches from the man's foot, he kneels beside it to get a better look. Inspecting it carefully, the man lifts it into his hand as he starts to look at the brown paper cylinder as specks start to spew out the side of it.

"Que es?" one of the guards asks, shifting the attention of the other.

"Es un cigarro," the other replies as he looks back at the smoke as it starts to retreat out of the building. Then before either can make another move, another shadow appears from the smoke as it sends the two men back another couple of steps. Drawing them to the next level of downward stairs, they watch on as the shadow gets closer.

"Amigo?" one of the guards asks as they watch the shadow continue to approach the edge of the shadowy realm. Then after a couple of more seconds, they watch in fear as two balls of orangish light appear from the top of the shadow.

"Salgamos de aqui," the other guard yells as they turn their attention toward the stairs. Before they can begin to make a run for it, the shadow within the smoke disappears as the two look on in confusion. Looking at one another, they once more take a glance at the retreating smoke to find no sign of any figure. Foot after foot, the smoke dissipates, leaving nothing behind besides ash and coal covering the platform above them. Gulping down some confidence, one of the men makes his way carefully toward the exit as he starts to peek his head through the dark doorway. However just as he is about to lookout a bright flash rings out, sending him trembling behind the wall.

The glow reflecting off the fading paint, he watches as it dims before turning to the other guard as he remains on the platform between the stairs. As their eyes make contact, the guard turns his attention back to the doorway in time to see the night swallow up the last few remnants. With the smoke clear, the guard looks down at the spots of ash along the broken cement before he slides his back along the wall. Coming to a seating position, he looks over at the pile closest to him before cracking his thumbs. Placing his head back on the wall, the sound of footsteps echoes throughout.

"Utilizar esta," the other guard says, turning the attention of the other. Seeing him, he throws a pistol toward the man as it bounces into his lap. Nodding his head, the man grabs the gun just in time to hear the footsteps stop. Cautiously turning his head back to the doorframe, he once again pokes his head out to see the empty rooftop to his surprise. Then with a massive breath, he climbs back to his feet when he starts to turn the gun toward the opening. As the man watches on, the guard steps out into the opening before taking a tiny step out into the darkness. With the light from the guard tower still swaying about, the man looks around the rooftop with no trace of Esteban as he continues to approach the edge. Placing his hands flat against the concrete, he looks over the edge before shifting his sight to the sky above.

Watching as the clouds start to shift through the moon, he finds nothing out of the ordinary when suddenly the sounds of footsteps start once more. This time as he stands in the aura of the light from the building, he watches as a singular massive shadow blocks it out. Picking the gun up, he turns around and starts to aim only to have his eyes widen when he sees the other man as his hand remains still along the door frame.

"No puedes hacer eso," the man replies as he lowers the gun as the other guard takes a step out onto the rooftop.

"Ambos sabemos que nunca le has disparado a nadie," the guard replies as he brushes off the man as he starts to venture closer to him.

"Si, pero podria haberlo hecho," the man replies as he continues to look around when suddenly the door shuts. Extinguishing most of the streams of light, the two men gather up as they keep their back toward the edge of the roof. Facing off, they watch as a shadow darts through the tiny strands of light. Seeing the shadow pass through, the man lifts the gun before firing a couple of shots in the direction of the door. Making no connection, the men stare at the tiny holes left behind as a series of footsteps echo over the sounds of helicopters flying throughout.

"Donde esta Col. Lins?" Esteban asks mysteriously through the darkness.

Searching for the source, the two men try to gather themselves as they look around the empty rooftop.

"No te lo vamos a decir," the guard replies as the other man nods in agreement.

"Respuesta incorrecta," Esteban's voice rings out once more as with the pass of a light from the guard tower it reveals him standing along the railing. Momentarily seeing his shadow appear in front of them, the men suddenly turn around as once more the darkness swallows up the rooftop. As the two men struggle to search for Esteban, the door behind them swings open with an obnoxious screech. Turning their attention, the man's hand nervously shakes the gun as they cautiously take a step forward. Aiming the gun toward it, he turns his attention toward the other man who gulps down some saliva before nodding his head.

Shifting his gaze back to the door, a sudden commotion catches his attention when he watches as the man goes sliding down onto the dusty floor. Stopping feet from between the door and the other guard, he looks back as once again the light passes over the rooftop. This time the man catches eye contact with Esteban as his fiery gaze starts to overtake the darkness. Pulling the gun on Esteban, he unloads another couple of rounds as Esteban launches himself into the sky. Disappearing among the floating clouds, the man turns back to his friend who remains on the ground. Running over to him, he places his hand up against the side of his neck as his eyes search the sky. Then from out of the clouds, flames snake through the sections before turning downward. Spiraling around a red trail, flames spin downward as in front of it remains Esteban in flight.

The man's eyes widen as he rises to his feet before charging toward the open doorway. Leaving his friend behind, the man arrives at the door and cuts the corner before turning back to see his friend. Gathering his breath, the man shakes his head as he rises to his feet. Placing his hands on the sides of his head, the man shakes the cobwebs free once more when he sees the man hiding back inside.

"Donde esta?" the guard asks as he looks at the man cowering in the doorway. However, before he can answer, the glow of the flames start to reflect off the dirty rooftop. Turning his attention upward, the man screams as suddenly Esteban and the spiraling funnel of flames crashes down upon him. Silencing his screams, the flames roar before dissipating into the darkness. Leaving nothing behind but a pile of ash, the man trembles in fear as he sees Esteban looking down at the results of his attack.

Dropping the gun, the clang shifts Esteban's attention as flames from within his gaze intensifies with each passing second.

"Se dirige hacia la tienda de dulces," the man squeals as he drops to his knees.

"Que es la tienda de dulces?" Esteban asks as he takes a couple of steps toward the man.

"Asi es como llama a su yate ya que contiene todos los bienes que roba," the man replies as he starts to weep before dropping his head in sadness.

"Donde encuentro esta tienda de dulces?" Esteban replies as he continues to bring himself closer to the man. Sobbing uncontrollably, the man wipes his face one side at a time before turning upward to see him stop just feet from him. Before he can speak a word, he watches Esteban squat down as he stares the man in his eyes. Placing his hand on the man's shoulder, he nods as the man signals back with an understanding.

"Bahia de la Habana," the man mutters as Esteban closes his eyes before turning his attention toward the edge of the rooftop. Releasing his hold on the man's shoulder, he turns back before taking a pair of steps when he hears the man get back to his feet. Before either of them can say another word, footsteps start to charge up from the building when a group of guards appear from behind the man. Pushing him aside, the squad prepares to unleash when suddenly the man stands in front of them.

"Antes de disparar por lo menos dime donde está mi hijo?" Esteban asks as once more the flames start to quell from the depths of his irises. Seeing the flames rise through his chest, the man continues to hold up his hand as he turns to him.

"Ni una palabra mas soldado," one of the soldiers replies as he takes off the safety from his rifle. One by one, the others do the same as this time the man in front of them stands dead center with his arms out wide.

"Tu hijo esta en la tienda pero tu amigo esta aquí en una celda," the man shouts out as one of the soldiers lowers his gun before breaking rank.

"Mi amigo?" Esteban replies as his eyes widen watching as the soldier comes forth and grabs hold of the man as he tries to break free.

"Hable otra palabra y serás castigado," the soldier says as he kicks the man to the ground. Placing his hands above his head, the man looks over at Esteban as he once more tries to get free.

"Si, Loca Manzana," the man yells when suddenly the soldier behind him points to Esteban as suddenly the rest of the group press their triggers. Before their bullets can release, the soldier tosses the man to the side to clear their path. With every squeeze of the trigger, bullets start to fly as Esteban charges ahead of them. Heading toward the swirling lights from the watch tower, he dives off the rooftop as the bullets pass over him. Continuing to fire with diminishing hopes, the soldier looks over at the man on the floor with a snarl on his face.

Then with a callous look over his face, the soldier pulls out his gun and points it at the man.

"Por favor Hector dejame ir somos hermaños," the man pleas with his hands out in front of him. His palms facing Hector, he watches as he lowers the gun before turning to the other men as they start to run for the edge of the rooftop. With their guns out front, they stand at the edge looking over, leaving Hector and the man by themselves.

"Corre Antonio antes de que cambie de opinión," Hector says as he sees Antonio from the corner of his eyes. With little thought, he watches as Antonio gets up and starts to take off for the doorway. Meanwhile, Hector's mind starts to race as his finger starts to hover over the pristine metal of the trigger.

"Ven conmigo," Antonio's voice rings out which causes Hector's eyes to squeeze out a tear. Before the droplet can hit the ground, he turns to the man as he stands in the middle of the opening.

"No puedo," Hector replies as he shakes the gun at his side.

"Por qué hermaño?" Antonio asks as he motions his hands toward the staircase. Then without a word, he watches as Hector lifts the gun and aims it at him, forcing Antonio's hands up in the air.

"Eres una traidor a la causa," Hector says as he pulls the trigger, which lets loose a round. As another tear attempts to slide down his cheek, the bullet strikes Antonio in the center of his chest. The force of the strike sending him into the wall behind him, life starts to fade from his body as blood starts to fall from the wound. Struggling to gasp for a breath, Antonio lifts his hand to the hole as he starts to feel the warmth of the blood rushing out.

"Lo lament," Antonio cries as his hand lowers back to his side as he struggles to move.

"TRAIDOR," Hector yells as he fires another shot, which hits just inches from the first wound. As his eyes close, Hector watches as Antonio's legs buckle as he tumbles down the staircase out of sight of the rooftop. Once the smoke swirls from the muzzle of the gun, he drops it to the ground before turning to see the others who continue their search. Running up from behind them, he finds an open spot before beginning his own search. Finding nothing alongside the rest of the group, they all turn back and start to head back inside. As they approach the open doorway, Hector looks back at the edge of the rooftop once more.

CHAPTER 12

As he stands in silence even as the others start to charge through the trail of blood along the floor, Esteban floats downward as he continues to search for an opening back inside. Splitting plumes of smoke on his way down, his eyes catch sight of a massive opening along the segments of concrete. Getting closer, he spots the shards of broken glass and remnants of wood everywhere when it hits him. This debris came from the room where he had been once before. As he approaches the space, he discovers it to from where he and Loca Manzana had taken hold in. Just before he can fall past it, he extends his arms out as it allows his hands to connect with the shards of the broken metal shards hanging off the cement. Avoiding any sharp edge, Esteban grabs hold as his momentum stops. Then with a single lift, he floats up and over the edge before placing his feet down safely.

"Eso estuvo cerca," Esteban says as he once more looks around the room before catching sight of a cigar sitting along the counter. Making his way over, he then blows a gentle stream of flames at the end of it. Once it starts to glow, he places the other end into his mouth before taking in an inhalation. As the embers spill onto the floor, the sounds of footprints once more ring out. Coming from down the hallway, Esteban dodges the line of sight as the patrol guards head down the hall.

"Nosotros necesitamos llegar a la prisión," one of the soldiers shout from the front. As the others roar in unison, they charge down the hall and around the corner as Esteban peeks out just in time to see the last one disappear. As the man's shadow shrinks along the wall, Esteban throws the cigar out of the opening before heading out of the doorway. Checking both ways before committing, he turns the way the guards are heading when he begins to charge down the path. After a couple of mighty steps, he leaps around the corner to see a beige door with a rusty door handle. With a single flick of the wrist, he opens the creaking door before stepping into the room. Finding levels upon levels of staircases, sounds of footsteps echo out as he turns his attention to the first set of stairs.

"Como has llegado hasta aquí?" a voice rings out feet from the stairs as the sounds of a round of ammunition entering the chamber rings out.

Esteban drops down as the series of bullets fire out as they strike the wall, blasting plaster all over the floor. Hearing the silence return, the sounds of footsteps cause Esteban to rise back to his feet. Seeing the man just feet from him, the man once again attempts to reload his weapon. As Esteban charges forward, the man takes aim as his finger slides over the trigger. Then just as he goes to squeeze it, Esteban grabs the weapon before snatching it from the man's grasp. With an effortless toss, the weapon goes out of the doorway as it clangs against the cold stone floor.

After watching the gun bounce off the ground, the man swings mightily as Esteban's jaw. Whiffing through the air, the man turns back only to be on the receiving end of a forearm from Esteban. Dropping to his knee, the man unhooks a knife from under his boot as his other arm rubs against his face.

"Pagaras por eso," the man replies before attempting to stab Esteban. Trying to make multiple attempts, Esteban dodges each one until he is back first with the guard rail. As his breath turns heavy, the man yells as he charges Esteban with his knife high into the sky.

"O puedes decime lo que quiero saber," Esteban replies, grabbing hold of the man's arm as it stops in its tracks. With both arms around the mans', he charges forward before crashing the man's back into the cement wall. Hitting square between the bullet holes, the man releases the knife as it drops onto the floor.

"Ay por favor tu eres el gran héroe Tormenta Cubano", the man chuckles when suddenly Esteban places his arm against the man's throat. Placing his own hands up against Esteban's massive arm, he struggles to gather a breath as the man starts to lose the color on his skin.

"Si y tienes a mi hijo y mi amigo," Esteban replies as he feels a breath struggle to make its way down the man's throat. Then as his eyes start to roll back, he weakens the pressure to allow the man to regain consciousness. As his feet drop softly to the ground, he starts to wheeze and cough. Dropping down to the ground on all fours, he crawls about before pushing himself up to a squatting position.

"Tu hijo no esta aquí," the man replies before letting out another round of coughing. Before Esteban can reply, he starts to stand back up as he brushes himself clean of the dirt and dust along the ground.

"Lo sé pero donde esta mi amigo?" Esteban asks as this time he grabs him by the collar of his shirt. Picking him up once more so his feet can sway about the ground, the man stares into Esteban's eyes as a round of tears fall from his eyes.

"Esta dos pisos mas abajo de aquí," the man replies to Esteban's surprise as he releases his hold. Allowing the man the freedom to return to the ground, he fixes his collar before wiping his eyes free from the straying tears that remain along his cheeks. Watching as Esteban shifts his attention, the man pulls the knife from the floor from underneath his shirt. Continuing to listen to the footsteps as their echoes fade, Esteban approaches the guardrail with both hands around it. As he keeps his focus outward, the man cautiously steps closer as he tries to attempt to minimize the echoes. Getting to about a foot from Esteban, the man lifts his knife into the air as he prepares to deal a death blow.

"Voy a verte pronto," Esteban mumbles as he tightens his grasp around the guardrail.

"Eres demasiado confiado en tu poder," the man replies as he starts to swing down his knife. Before Esteban can turn his attention, a gunshot rings out as a groan squeals out. Hearing the thud from behind him, Esteban turns back to see a soldier from the doorway with a smoking gun in its hand. Looking for the other, Esteban's eyes shift down to the ground to see the man groaning as he lays flat on his stomach. With the knife inches from his cooling hand, blood starts to puddle up from the wound along his back. Kicking the knife down the stairs, Esteban turns to the soldier as he lowers the gun back into the holster.

"Gracias?" Esteban says as he watches the soldier make his way inside toward the man's body. Placing fingers along the man's neck, the soldier stands back up before lifting the hat that sat upon its head. Revealing the flowing brown hair, the soldier lowers the mask covering its face to reveal its feminine features. More importantly, this was no ordinary women, instead it was one that Esteban knows from his past.

"De nada," she replies as she clears the shell casing from out of the gun. Hearing it clang along the ground, Esteban watches as she steps into the streaks of moonlight coming in from the far wall.

"Que haces aqui Roxana?" Esteban asks as she smirks before turning her attention back to him.

"Para buscar mi amor," Roxanne replies as she places the hat back over her head. Turning the safety back on, she places the gun back before looking toward the staircase.

"Como supiste donde estaba?" Esteban asks as he takes a couple of steps closer to her.

"Los disparos pero de todos modos lo vamos a rescatar," Roxanne answers as he approaches the top step of the staircase. With a nod, they approach the top step before he watches Roxanne poke her head over the guardrail. Joining her, they watch as the last guard steps off the staircase and approaches the open doorway.

"Vamos a buscarlo," Esteban whispers when suddenly the man beneath them stops in his tracks. Taking a step back, he looks up at the two of them before pointing his rifle upward. After unloading a couple of rounds in their direction, the two of them duck downward as the bullets ricochet off the plaster. Once the final shot was fired, footsteps start to echo about as Esteban attempts to get a tiny peek. Seeing a pair of other guards charging up the stairs, he kneels back down and turns to Roxanne as she scoots over to the edge of the wall. Leaving an inch between herself and the stairs, she places herself flat against the plaster as she holds her gun to her chest.

As the first guard makes his way to the last step of the stairs, they watch as he steps onto the platform. Before he makes the turn, gunfire shoots out as Roxanne fires a shot into the man's leg causing him to hold his leg in shock. Blood starting to release as he loosens his grip on his weapon, Esteban suddenly charges forward and tackles him into the wall. Dropping the gun on the floor, Esteban grabs the man by the shoulders before throwing him into the other guard standing alone on the staircase. Watching as they tumble downward , two gun shots smash into the drywall inches from Esteban's face. Looking at the bottom of the staircase, Esteban watches as a guard lowers his rifle as the scope aims to the floor. Making eye contact, Esteban then steps back as flames start to rise from the depths of his sternum.

After a couple of seconds, the two guards crash down onto the platform, feet from the last guard who lowers the gun to his side. Momentarily shifting his sight to the two guards groaning in pain beside him, the guard turns his attention to see smoke start to swirl from between Esteban's nostrils. Without a spoken word, Esteban screams before charging toward the railing as it lifts Roxanne to her feet. Uncertain of what to do, she watches on as Esteban dives over the railing as an explosion of flames combusts from thin air. Spinning like a tornadic cyclone, the flames proceed downward, burning the plaster all around the staircase.

Fear swallowing up the man's eyes, he darts outward as the two others start to come too. Catching sight of the intensifying glow, they shake their dizziness loose before stumbling out behind him. Just as they get to the doorway, Esteban slams down on his knee as the flames erupt upward as they bounce off the bottom platform. Brushing Roxanne on their way up, Esteban turns his attention to see her poke her head from beyond the guardrail. As the flames dissipate along the ceiling, she looks upward before turning her attention back to the staircase. Making her way downward, Esteban shifts his attention toward the retreating men as they continue down an empty hall.

Taking a step, his foot smacks into the rifle left behind by one of the guards. Catching his attention, he kneels, and grabs hold of it before turning his attention back to the men as they stop just shy of the opposite end of the hall. Tilting his head to the side, he looks back at the men before tossing the gun off to the side. Smirking as the flames remain stagnant along his collarbones, he takes a couple of steps forward. Trembling in fear, the guards push and shove each other until finally one of them reaches for the doorknob to push it open. Breaking it free from the hinges, the guards charge through and head into the darkness of the hallway behind it.

Watching as their shadows disappear, Esteban stops in the entrance of the hall before turning back as he hears the clanging of footsteps. Looking, he sees Roxanne make her way over to the rifle as she leaves a trail of prints behind in the sections of ash along the ground. Reaching downward, she places the rifle over her back and turns her attention back to Esteban. With a nod, she makes her way past him before passing a couple of doors. Opening the first one on her left, they find themselves inside an empty office with a tiny Russian flag beside a large computer monitor. Along the edge of the counter sits a tiny glass with a minuscule amount of brown liquid. Bubbles cautiously making their way to the surface as they dodge the dissolving ice, Roxanne approaches it before wrapping her hand around it.

"Esto no es aqua," Roxanne says as she starts to swirl the liquid. Watching as a thin foam starts to grow along the top, Esteban steps inside beside her. Looking at the glass within her grasp, something along the wall catches his attention as he shifts his gaze. In front of him, he takes in a massive map of Cuba as Florida sits just to the north. Along with the usual landmarks throughout the island, red Xs sit throughout the image. Then as Esteban's eyes drift northward, his eyes catch sight of one X. Located overtop the northern side of the image this one was not over any part of Cuba. Instead, it was over the tip of the Florida Keys. Placing his finger on the map where they are and sliding it upward to the northern most X, Esteban turns to Roxanne as she places the glass back where it was.

"Que esta planeando?" Esteban asks before turning his attention to where his finger stops along the map.

"No se," Roxanne replies before making her way around the desk before pulling out the dark leather chair. Sitting on it as she rolls forward, she starts to look down at the keyboard in front of her. Seeing one of the keys up top missing from the rest, she moves the mouse as it turns the screen away from the black screensaver before revealing the image behind it. However even with the veil taken away, the desktop remains hidden when she looks down again at the keyboard. Moving her hand over top, she finds herself frozen over a missing key to the right of the 'F8' key.

"Lo que esta mal?" Esteban asks as he turns his attention over to her as she starts to search for the missing key. Watching as she checks every square inch of the desk and the crevices, they start to throw the assorted items around the computer onto the floor. Suddenly her attention shifts to the top drawer along the filing cabinet beside the mouse. After pulling it open, she surfs the various folders when suddenly Esteban watches her hands stop between a pair near the back of the drawer. Reaching inside, she pulls out a black key and places it along the missing spot in the keyboard.

"Vamos a ver que esconde," Roxanne replies as he starts to press the button. With each press, the screen gets lighter until finally the image starts to reveal itself. Seeing what is appearing before them, the two start to see a scene of still water. As the image remains frozen, details become clearer as the picture adjusts to the quality of the monitor. However just before they can continue, a loud bang echoes through the walls. Forcing Roxanne to push herself back from the keyboard, Esteban looks over at the open doorway. Once she gets to her feet, they turn to each other when another rumble echoes around them. Placing his hand out in front of her, Esteban balls up his other hand before making his way toward the opening.

"Que es?" Roxanne asks as she tries to look past Esteban toward the open hallway.

Watching in silence, Esteba turns his head before looking in both directions seeing no trace of anyone. Finally, he steps out completely before stopping dead center as Roxanne comes out of the room. As they both stand in the middle, another thunderous rumble echoes out which causes them to charge forward. Stopping just down the hall, the two approach the source as it hides behind a plain, white door. To the right of the door handle sits an automatic pin pad with a scanner in the center.

"Apuesto a que lo que estamos buscando esta detras de la Puerta numero uno," Esteban says as he places his hand over the scanner.

However, before Roxanne responds, the door behind them opens wide which forces them to turn around.

"Quien esta aqui?" the soldier replies as he steps toward the open doorway with gun drawn.

"Sal de camino," Esteban says as he turns his attention momentarily to Roxanne as she turns toward the open office beside the man.

"INTRUSO," the man screams as he squeezes the trigger as Roxanne charges toward the office door. Then as her foot gets to the edge of the door frame, bullets start to ring out as she dives out of the way. Racing behind the desk in the room, the bullets echo about as Esteban charges down the hallway. One by one, they make an impact with the walls as spurts of plaster flare out until finally Esteban dives onto the floor. Unloading another shot, the man steps out from the doorway before turning to Esteban. Shaking the ringing from his ears, Esteban turns to see the man as bullet shells pile along the ground.

CHAPTER 13

Meanwhile in the room, Roxanne dives out of view as her hands grab a firm hold on the area around the keyboard. Picking herself up, her hands press down on some of the buttons as she stands back up. Avoiding any sight of the man, she stands still in the space between the computer desk and the doorway. Keeping a focus on her breath, the sound from the screen starts up as the waves on the image start to move about. Reaching over to silence the audio, she squats down as from the silence, she starts to hear the footsteps once more. Closing her eyes as her body starts to shake in fear, another gunshot rings about the room. Tears flowing down her cheeks as a thud shivers the floor, she prepares herself to poke her head into the open doorway. Then as she goes to extend out, a body flies through the wall before colliding with the space beneath a tiny window.

The impact reverberating the entire office causes the map to fall onto the floor as it effectively covers the body. Roxanne then starts to make her way over when she pulls down the section over the top of the body. Revealing an unfamiliar face, she scoots back as another shadow approaches from out of the doorway. Turning her attention to the opening, relief settles over her as she sees Esteban without a wound with his hand settling overtop the doorframe.

"Estas herido?" Roxanne asks as she watches Esteban take a couple steps into the room.

"Ni siquiera me toco," Esteban replies with a smile as he approaches the man's body. Squatting beside Roxanne, he reaches over and closes the man's eyes before pulling the map further to inspect the man's coat once more. After checking the various pockets along the man's jacket, he finds an ID badge hiding inside of the last one.

As he is searching, Roxanne takes a glance over to the open hallway, seeing the broken shards of drywall and bullet fragments that pile up on the ground. However, seeing no trace of blood anywhere, she turns to see Esteban as he finally pulls out the badge. Turning her attention, Esteban hands it over to her as he starts to get back to his feet. Then as she follows suit, something on the computer screen catches their attention. Gone was the image of the frozen waves and instead was a shifting look of the ocean with rocks protruding from the surface. Above those is a cement guardrail with a single object rising above the gray barrier. Entering the bluish gray sky above, the item with various shades of color stands as drops of sea foam remain frozen in the image.

"Que es eso?" Esteban asks as he points over to the screen.

"Nada que haya visto aqui en Cuba," Roxanne replies as she presses the same button as before. Playing the video, the sight shifts closer to the monument as it zooms in overtop the shifting currents below. Even as the waves contact the rocks, the camera remains steady around an empty boardwalk along the street. Seeing the various layers on the object become more distinct, the clouds above break apart as more of the details start to come into view. Then as it motions to the opposite side that faces the street, the camera stops with the object in the center. Then as Roxanne and Esteban continue to watch, the object splits from the platform below. Allowing steam to escape, the sides split wider, revealing the darkness hiding behind it. Once they stop moving as the mist from the crashing waves rise overtop, the camera shoots inside when suddenly the image turns black.

"Es eso?" Esteban asks to Roxanne as she motions the mouse over to the bottom left of the image.

"Eso creo," Roxanne replies as she nods her head. Before either of them can say another word, another thud echoes out which sends them back into the hallway. Turning back to the doorway with the keypad by its side, the two approach it as Roxanne steps closer. As her hands start to shake in front of the sensor, she struggles to keep the badge still as the red light on the sensor turns black. After a couple of seconds of nervousness, the light returns green as the automatic lock on the door pops free. Releasing the door from the frame, Esteban walks over and pulls it wider. Revealing the darkness within, he squints his eyes as a smirk starts to come over his emotionless face. Before saying a word, he steps inside the room as Roxanne looks on in uncertainty.

"Mi amigo es que to estas ahi?" Esteban says from the darkness as Roxanne prepares herself to step into the fading darkness.

"Ya es hora de que aparezca la poderosa, Tormenta Cubano," responds the other voice which sends Roxanne further inside the room. Getting closer to Esteban as he stands a foot away, Roxanne flips a switch along the wall as the lights along the roof turn on. Once it completely illuminates, Roxanne smiles as she sees Mario standing beside the window. Bruises and blood drying along his five o'clock shadow, Mario looks back with a grin as she charges toward the cage door.

"Estas vivo," Mario mutters as she places her hand between the metal bars. Extending past the door, their hands come together as the fingers interlock as their eyes meet. Tears flowing down toward their cheeks, they wipe them off as Mario turns his attention to Esteban.

"El me trajo a ti," Roxanne replies, switching Mario's attention back to her.

"Despues de que ella me salvo," Esteban says, turning his attention back to him.

"Es possible que no quieras decirle eso en voz alta al senor heroe," Mario replies as he turns his attention back to Esteban. Sneering his upper lip as Roxanne smirks, Esteban steps toward the cage door before looking down at the metallic handle. Reaching for the knob, Esteban grabs hold before watching his chest and arm start to glow. Then as the fire starts to brew within, the muscles and veins start to tighten as his hand tightens around the metal. As the handle starts to shake, it pops off the door with one sudden twist as he flings it against the wall. Smashing against the stones before flopping to the ground, Esteban and Roxanne turn their attention back to the door.

"¿Bien, cuál es tu plan ahora? Roxanne asks, motioning toward the broken joint where the doorknob once sat.

"Mario da un paso atras," Esteban replies before balling his hand up into a fist.

Watching as Mario cautiously steps out of the way, Roxanne watches as Esteban twists his hips before pulling his arm back. Then with the force of a Caribbean storm, his fist slams into the rusty metallic bars along the cage door. As the metal starts to reverberate and tremble, the force breaks the hinges holding it in place. Sliding across the floor, the door slides to a stop before leaning up against the wall beside the sole window. With their eyes wide, the two look on when Esteban turns to Roxanne.

Struggling to figure out the next move, Esteban looks over at Mario and points before turning his attention to Roxanne.

Meanwhile, Roxanne's attention shifts to Mario as a grin swiftly appears when she starts to charge forward.

Readying for her embrace, his arms spread open as she comes closer when the two make impact. Mario's arms wrap around her as they embrace as Esteban looks away. Taking a step toward the shelving, the two step back before turning their attention back to Esteban.

"Gracias por encontrarme," Mario says as he turns his focus to Esteban as once more Roxanne starts to hug him tightly.

"Ojala mi hijo estuviera aqui," Esteban replies as he angrily punches a hole in the center of the cabinet sitting just above the counter. As the white wood snaps in pieces all over the ground, Esteban places his hands on the wooden counter before placing his head in the center.

Beginning to sob, his breathing intensifies as his legs start to wobble beneath him. Before anyone can speak another word, the room starts to shake and tremble as they turn their attention toward the open window. Hearing an orchestra of sounds, the trio make their way over to the glass panels to try to get a better look. Hearing the pulling of gears, they turn their attention in time to see a massive yacht slide from underneath their location. Watching as it makes its way around the walkway, they watch as it clears the building. Once fully into view, the room shakes once more as a group of guards appear into view. Standing still on the wooden pier, they stand at attention when suddenly their attention shifts down the path.

"Mira, ahi esta el," Mario says as he places a finger between a set of smudges along the glass. He then turns to Roxanne and Esteban as they try to clear the window to get a better view. After a couple of moments, they spot him once he steps further away from the shadow of the building. Watching on, the guards salute the man as he makes his way in front of two guards as they hold another.

"Como llegamos alli?" Roxanne asks as she steps from the window.

Before Mario can speak, Esteban turns his back to the window before taking a couple of steps toward the empty doorway of the cage.

Turning around, he looks at the window first before switching over to the remains of the door that leans against the wall beside them. With a grin he starts to prepare himself to charge at it when suddenly a jolt of pain starts to take control of his body. Dropping to his knees, his hand reaches to his side as both Roxanne and Mario look on with eyes wide open. Uncertain of the next move, they watch Esteban pull up his shirt before revealing the light shirt beneath as blood starts to stain the fabric. Taking the shirt completely off before throwing it on the floor, he then pulls up the other to reveal the wound site. Seeing the mixture of dry and fresh blood, the wound starts to grow and swell as Esteban continues to grimace in pain.

As Mario remains frozen in uncertainty, Roxanne charges forward to Esteban's side before looking at the wound as she pulls back the military vest from off her shoulders.

"Que crees que estas haciendo?" Mario asks as he tries to get a better look. Not responding, Roxanne looks over at the corner shelving as she spots some medical grade items that sit along with the broken pieces of wood. Going over to it, she pulls out a syringe and some bandages.

"Ademas da ser portador de aqua, Tambien soy enfermero," Roxanne replies as she gathers up the ítems. Then turning her attention to Esteban as the items remain in her hands, she lays the stuff down atop a piece of wood that had made its way over.

"Sera major que te apures estan a punto de llegar al yate," Mario says as he turns his head from the window beside him. Watching as Roxanne runs over to the shelving and clears off the debris, Mario turns to Esteban as his reddening eyes look over at him.

"Aqui no hay medicina," Roxanne yells as she slams one of the cabinet doors shut.

"Como te dispararon?" Mario asks Esteban as he looks over his shoulder at Roxanne who continues to search the ruble. He then turns back to Mario who nods his head before placing his hand down on Esteban's shoulder.

"Necesito encontrar elixir Cubano," Esteban replies softly as Mario turns to Roxanne who swipes her hand, sending the last bits of wood onto the floor.

"El necesita azucar," Mario says as Roxanne turns her attention to him before looking at the open doorway to the main room.

"Dejame revisar la habitacion al otro lado del pasillo," Roxanne replies as she starts to run out and into the hall.

Hearing her rummage through the various rooms, Mario turns to Esteban as he continues to normalize his breathing to prevent further weakness.

"Como sabes lo que es un yate?" Esteban asks as he looks up at the sky before turning his attention to Mario who smirks in response.

"Siempre he Sabido cosas aleatorias como que vas a romper esa pared," Mario replies before turning his attention as the sound of footsteps start to get closer. Watching as a shadow grows along the wall, Esteban turns in time to see Roxanne reappear with a Styrofoam cup as steam rises from out of the lid.

Approaching the two men, Roxanne turns to Esteban before he turns his attention back to her.

"Todo lo que pude encontrar fue este café," Roxanne says as she places it down along the cement floor beside the syringe.

"Mi amor eso es elixir Cubano," Mario replies as he momentarily looks over at Esteban who is shaking his head.

"Como beber esto va a ayudar a su herida?" Roxanne asks as she pops off the lid allowing the steam to swirl in the air around them. Sending a strong smell into the stale air, Roxanne looks over at Mario who turns to her while Esteban drops his shoulders.

"El no lo esta bebiendo," Mario answers as he looks down at the syringe beside the swirling brown liquid beside it. Following his lead, Roxanne follows his gaze downward until it stops at the syringe. Realizing what he was going to ask her to do, her gaze switches back to his as he turns his focus back to her.

"No puedo hacerlo," Roxanne says as she gets back up with her arms out wide and her head shaking negatively.

"Tienes que hacerlo allo mismo," Mario replies as he points to an area just above where the wound is located. Pushing a little too hard, Esteban grimaces in pain which causes him to look over at him.

"Cuidado con tus dedos regordetes," Esteban mutters.

"No le hará daño?" Roxanne asks as she takes a step closer to them.

"Nos mataria a nosotros pero a el no," Mario replies as he turns to Esteban who looks at Roxanne before nodding his head as confirmation.

"Bien aqui va," Roxanne replies as she kneels before peeling the plastic off the syringe.

Mario and Esteban await her next move as they watch the plastic slide onto the ground. They then watch as she dips the needle into the brownish liquid before pulling up on the plunger. With every inch, liquid enters the chamber as it passes each line with ease. Once the amount is correct, Roxanne lifts it up as it allows a couple of drops to fall back into the cup. Once the last drop filters out, she then turns the needle upward before examining the storage. To remove the air from within the syringe, she gently pushes the plunger as the coffee starts to compress. Then as they start to see beads of coffee form at the end of the needle, she stops before shaking the last droplet free.

"Esta listo para ir?" Mario asks, shifting Roxanne's attention momentarily before she nods her head.

Watching as her attention shifts to Esteban's wound, she gulps down some confidence, aiming the needle toward him. Cautiously making her way in his direction, the needle shakes inches from the wound along with her hand. Then just as it gets within centimeters from his skin, she pulls it back and exhales deeply.

"No lo soporto con café," Roxanne cries as she lowers her head.

"Esta bien solo respire por un segundo," Mario replies as he steps closer before giving her a hug. As he consoles her, the syringe remains tight in her grasp as Esteban looks down at his wound.

Struggling to keep the bleeding from worsening, Esteban places his hand over the bandage before turning to them.

"No para romper tu tiempo pero estoy sangrando aquí," Esteban says as the two split before turning their attention toward him.

"No ves que esta estresada?" Mario asks angrily as he steps between the two of them.

"Lo hago pero necesito salvar a mi hijo," Esteban replies as Mario backs down before turning his attention to Roxanne as she stares at the syringe to her side.

Gulping down another ounce of nervousness, she attempts another step toward him when suddenly the horn from the ship rings out.

Sending them toward the window, they watch as Mario charges toward the glass to watch as Col. Lins along with Esteban's son make their way past the guards. As his attention remains, Esteban gingerly makes his way over to Roxanne as he removes his hand from the wound. Extending his palm upwards to her, the blood starts to stain his hand as he looks over.

"Dejame hacer esto," Esteban whispers as she looks down at the syringe.

Pausing for a moment, she then nods before placing the syringe into his hand. Wrapping it in his grasp, she pulls away as she retreats a step before turning her attention to Mario.

"Donde estan ellos?" Roxanne asks before turning to Esteban who then looks down at the syringe within his hand.

"Estan justo dentro de la sombra del edificio," Mario replies as he turns to see her with both hands empty. Then before he can shift his attention, Esteban rams the syringe's needle deep into the skin just above the broken flesh. Letting out a scream, he pushes the plunger as it sends the coffee deep beneath the tissue and muscle. Once the final drop is inside, he drops the syringe before his muscles can start to spasm and drops to a knee. After a few seconds, they watch as Esteban rises to his feet as he rips off the bandage to reveal a section of unbroken skin. Without a drop of blood leaking out, he turns his attention back to the section of metal door that lay just feet from him. Shifting his gaze onto his arms as veins pulse toward his wrists and hands, he then flexes his fingers into a fist. After releasing his hands, he then turns toward the door once more with a sneer upon his face.

"Que estas pensando?" Roxanne asks as Mario turns his attention toward her before shifting back to Esteban.

"El va a entregar la fuerza de la tormenta Cubano," Mario replies with a gentle nod.

Before Roxanne can reply, steam starts to leak out from Esteban's nostrils as fire spirals into the core of his pupils. Then with the force of the caffeinated fluid swimming through his body, Esteban charges toward the metal door. Then just as he spears through its center, Mario pulls Roxanne back before wrapping her up in his arms. Bracing for impact, Esteban crashes into the door before exploding through the stone wall behind it. Leaping through the room and out into the humid Cuban air, Esteban soars through the air before catching sight of the door beneath him.

He then reaches out for it as he grabs hold of the metal pipes along the edges. Moving it over his head, Esteban continues to soar through the clouds as his eyes contact the pier as Col. Lins continues downward. As his hands bend the metal and his grip tightens, he shifts his descent before turning his attention to the group making their way toward the yacht awaiting them. Growing closer, he looks down at the pair of guards behind them when he sees his shadow developing along the wooden panels. Then before any of them can spot it, he launches the metal door forward as it accelerates toward them. Catching speed as it angles downward, Esteban's eyes shift colors as he launches a fire ball behind it. Colliding with the door, it engulfs the metal as it continues its path. Streaking through the sky, flames trail behind it as Esteban floats carefully behind it.

Meanwhile, back along the wooden pier, the guards turn their attention to the swishing waters beneath them. Suddenly they see a shadow grow beneath them, causing them to turn to Col. Lins who drags Rafael closer to the yacht's staircase. Before either of them can speak, their eyes catch a glow shining on them. Turning their attention back to the water, they watch as it pushes away from the dock as fish start to swim away. Feeling the heat intensify, the guards look up just as the flaming door crashes down on top of them before exploding the pier beneath them. Causing an explosion to shoot into the sky, steam starts to follow as the metal shards splash down into the bubbling current beneath.

Turning his neck at breakneck speed, Col. Lins looks back to see the embers shooting all over as he pushes Rafael inches from the first step.

Struggling to get back to his feet, Rafael turns to see Col. Lins approaching the wreckage as bits of wood crash down around him. Using his hand to block away some of the heat and light, he continues to approach the site when he stops as something catches his attention from among the clouds.

"Papa?" Rafael screams as they watch the blinding light rip through a pair of low floating clouds as they move across the sky.

Turning his attention momentarily to see the boy as he starts to sway his arms, Col. Lins emotions shift to anger as he motions his hands upward.

Seeing Col. Lins reaction, Rafael stops waving his arms as another shadow approaches from behind him. Grabbing his shoulder tightly, the person pulls Rafael back causing him to fall on his back along the bottom two stairs. Turning his eyesight toward the blue skies, he sees another guard with scars along his face as they split his goatee from left to right. Without notice, he starts to pull Rafael up the stairs as he strikes each edge on the way up. Getting closer to the yacht, the soldier stops for a moment to turn to Col. Lins before nodding his head. Smirking in response, he turns to look back at the incoming ball of light.

CHAPTER 14

As the speck starts to grow, the crackling of the flames melting through the wooden planks fade. Continuing to grow, the shadow becomes closer revealing Esteban's full figure. Spinning around as the flames shield him from all sides, he slows upon his approach. Getting closer to the deck, he lands as a plume of steam escapes from beneath his feet. Then with a crack of his neck, his body takes control as the flames start to retract. Returning into the core of his body, he flexes his muscles before looking back at the smoldering eruption between him and Col. Lins.

"LO DEJO IR," Esteban yells before taking a couple steps closer to Col. Lins.

Without a verbal response, Col. Lins picks up his hand into the air when suddenly the soldier drags up Rafael another step.

Letting out a wince, Esteban's eyes tighten with anger as he prepares to take another step. However just as his toes lift from the ground a series of clicks ring out, sending Esteban's sight behind him. Standing there, armed guards and soldiers drop to their knees with their rifles targeting him. Snickering at the men, he turns back to see Col. Lins who starts to smile. Watching with angst, he watches as Col. Lins starts to unbutton his colorful shirt from the bottom when suddenly he stops halfway. Revealing his muscular frame beneath, he turns to the soldier before turning his back on Esteban.

"Tienes el primer intent," Col. Lins says as he coughs a little.

"Que van a hacer mientras destruyo este heroico fraude?" the soldier asks, watching as Col. Lins continues to make his way up the stairs.

"Estare mirando mientras obtengo algo de mi adicción," Col. Lins replies as he scoots past Rafael before getting beside the soldier. After tapping him on the shoulder, Col. Lins yanks Rafael's arm so he rises back to his feet as the soldier makes his way down.

Step by step, the soldier loosens his fatigues as he stares a hole through Esteban. As the two men stares at each other waiting for the first move, the wind shifts directions as it comes off the ocean, sending the smoke clear of either man. Preparing for the first attack, the two pause as a crack echoes out causing them to look back at the staircase. Around the top, two guards bring Rafael out of sight as another stands at Col. Lins's side. Meanwhile within his grasp, an aluminum can which Col. Lins brings toward his mouth before slurping down a sip. Pulling it back from his lips, he places it to his side as he then looks down at the two men.

"Que estas esperando?" Col. Lins yells as the soldier nods his head before turning to Esteban who keeps his focus on the staircase.

"No te preocupes hijo ya voy," Esteban screams as fire once again builds within his sternum and pupils.

"Quien crees que eres?" the soldier asks as he removes his military jacket before pulling his machete out from his belt.

"Yo soy la Tormenta Cubano," Esteban yells back before something along the surface of the ocean catches his attention. A long section of sugarcane slaps into one of the large wooden posts along the sea, placing a smile on Esteban's face. Turning his attention back to the soldier in front of him, he dives into the ocean causing water to spread into the air. As droplets land throughout, the soldier charges forward seeing no trace of Esteban among the foamy surface currents. Looking up and down the rickety pier, he then turns back to Col. Lins as he tries to get a look at the ongoing scene.

"Lo ves a el?" Col. Lins asks before taking another sip from the can within his hand.

"No, creo que el pollo se escapo," the soldier replies before taking another look of the crashing seas. Seeing nothing once more, the soldier takes a couple of steps toward the staircase when suddenly the clouds overtop start to darken and tremble. As the rain starts to downpour, suddenly the winds start to return as steam rises from the misty breeze. Turning the man back, he watches as the surface of the sea starts to shift and spin. Then from within the depths of the sea, the water rises and churns as flames start to erupt.

Struggling to maintain its order, the water falls from all sides as the molten rock from the seafloor lifts upwards into the air as Esteban stands atop of it. With the piece of sugarcane within his grasp, he jumps off the solidifying platform and lands back atop the pier. Even as the rain continues to maul them, Esteban makes his way forward as he moves the shard to his side. With each step, steam rises from his skin as Esteban stands firm with the soldier in front of him. Before Esteban can make a move, the soldier looks over at the machete and then turns to Esteban. Then as the two men stand still, the soldier charges forward with the machete swinging high as Esteban prepares himself for a defensive.

Continuing his attack, Esteban stares on as flames start to cause his skin to glow. Channeling upwards through his sternum, the flames extend out into his arms and neck. Spiraling around the tensing muscles of his forearms, the embers turn their attention to the sugarcane as they spin up the stalk. Once they arrive up to the top, flames cascade toward his grasp as his eyes start to glow. Once they take hold, the soldier attempts to unleash the first strike. As the two strike each other, the reverberations send waves in all directions which causes the two men to skid in different directions.

Regaining their composure, the two men look at one another as the crackling flames continue to break the silence. Streaming smoke upward, the two men internally debate the next attack when the horn of the yacht behind them erupts from the speakers.

"Lo siento amigos pero esa es mi llamada," Col. Lins says as he tosses the empty glass out into the shifting currents below. Momentarily turning their attention, Col. Lins turns toward Rafael as he continues to struggle to get free. Picking him up with ease, he pushes him up the next few steps before disappearing from Esteban's sight. Following suit, Col. Lins stands atop the deck before saluting the men with a huge smile on his face.

"Te vencere," Esteban screams as steam starts to escape from his nostrils.

"Una ultima cosa," Col. Lins replies as he turns his attention toward the soldier as he looks over at his machete. Then with no response, the man charges toward a fraying piece of rope and splits it in half. As the machete remains within the fibers of the wood, the yacht turns free from the pier as the vibrations of the engine cause waves to kick up.

Sending mist and foam up into his face, Esteban struggles to move as the soldier charges up toward the stairs. One by one he climbs the steps as Esteban clears his eyes. Just as he makes it to the top, the staircase slides toward the edge of the pier when Esteban starts to charge toward the yacht. His feet blazing a path over the planks of woods, Esteban clenches his fists as he watches the soldier climb on the deck.

"Dispara ahora," the soldier yells before he and Col. Lins both disappear out of sight.

Then from out of the misty air behind him, the sounds of loading guns echo about as it causes Esteban to look back momentarily. Seeing the nozzles of the gun aiming at him, he turns his attention back to the staircase as it continues to get closer. Suddenly out of the fog, shots fire out in rapid procession as Esteban keeps his attention on the yacht as Col. Lins watches from the metal railing. One by one the bullets fly past him even as he continues his mission. Feeling a couple graze past him, he struggles to dodge them as the final one approaches him. As the last one zips past, he turns his attention toward the staircase as a rogue wave slam into the deck. After rocking the staircase for a few seconds, it then crashes into the side of the yacht before falling hopelessly into the angry waters below.

As the yacht continues to pull further away, Esteban starts to wobble and stumble as the effects of the caffeine start to wear off. So as a last ditch effort, he throws the burning stalk of sugarcane toward the hull of the boat. It then crashes into one of the windows along the lower level as it gets stuck in the center of the cracking glass. As steam and flames shoot and twist from just above the reach of the waves, Esteban watches on from the pier as the yacht gets further away.

"NO AHORA," Esteban screams as he attempts to lift from the vibrating planks along the deck. As his feet rise from the surface and into the air, the power fades as he drops back to the pier. Landing softly along the grains of wood, Esteban's jaw drops as he looks at his feet before turning toward the yacht. Then as he watches helplessly as the yacht rides the waves away, the clicks of loading guns catch his attention. Turning around, Esteban finds himself face to face with a squad of soldiers.

Barrels pointing in his direction, Esteban gulps before looking over his shoulder once more. Seeing the trail of fading smoke, he smirks before turning back to the squad of soldiers in front of him. Then after a couple of moments of tense staring, the soldiers lower their guns when two shadows step forward from the middle. Splitting the group, Esteban smirks as he spots Roxanne and Mario making their way forward.

"Nos extranaste?" Mario asks as he and Roxanne continue into the space between the two groups. Stopping just feet from Esteban, the two men hug before Esteban turns his attention back to the diminishing yacht.

"Puedes volar?" Roxanne asks as Esteban shifts his attention back to them. Shaking his head, Roxanne turns to Mario before looking back at Esteban once more.

"Estoy descafeinado," Esteban replies as he turns his attention back to the edge of the pier. Placing his hand down onto the algae-covered pier post, Esteban sits down as he allows his feet to sway back and forth in the open sea air. With the mist drifting into his face, Esteban stares out into the water as he watches the yacht disappear.

"Que Podemos hacer?" Roxanne asks as Esteban looks down before looking back over his shoulder.

"Necesito un bote y un café," Esteban replies.

"Bueno, no tengo un barco pero puedo ayudarte," one of the soldiers says as their attention shifts back to the group. Watching in surprise, one of the men lowers their weapon as Esteban turns toward him.

"Por qué deberiamos confiar en ti?" Roxanne asks as the soldier turns to her before momentarily turning his attention to the others.

"Tu Tambien tienes si quieres recuperar a tu hijo," the soldier replies when suddenly Esteban steps forward.

"Como te llamas?" Esteban asks, turning the attention of the soldier to him.

"Private Alvaro," the soldier replies before saluting the three of them.

"¿Privado, donde eres?" Esteban asks as Alvaro lowers his hand back down to his side.

"Santa Clara senor," Alvaro replies as he watches Esteban approach him before extending out his hand.

"Bienvenido a bordo," Esteban says as he reaches out his hand before connecting with Alvaro's hand. As the two men shake hands, he watches as Esteban turns back before nodding his head at both Roxanne and Mario. Reciprocating a nod, the two smirk and nod before approaching Alvaro as the other soldiers look on.

"Ven conmigo," Alvaro replies before turning his attention down the pier as he starts to make his way. As the rest of the group comes with him, they start to make their trek before turning the corner. Stepping off the wooden pier onto the solid ground, the group charges around the wall. Before them, the helicopter sits undamaged as the debris of gun shells and broken barrel sit throughout.

As Esteban stands next to Roxanne and Mario, Alvaro makes his way aboard before heading toward the cockpit.

Beginning to get things ready as the blades above start up, Esteban stands still before looking onto the ocean once more. Then with a deep breath, he turns back to the helicopter to see everyone sitting inside except for Mario.

"Vienes?" Mario asks as Esteban shifts his attention.

"Siento que me falta algo," Esteban replies before shrugging it off as he starts to make his way toward the helicopter.

"Eso es porque eres," Mario replies before turning Esteban's attention to him as his hand presses along the opening in the helicopter. Watching him, he then backs away before making his way back to him.

"Que es?" Esteban asks when suddenly Roxanne appears from her seat with a small Styrofoam cup in her hand.

"Tu café," Roxanne replies as Esteban's eyes focus on the cup in her hand. Without a word from Mario, Esteban makes his way toward the entrance of the helicopter as Roxanne moves out of the way. Clearing the path, he sits down beside the opening before grabbing hold of the cup. Popping off the lid, the steam from within rises toward their faces. As Mario stands on the outside, the blades of the motor speed up as the helicopter starts to rise off the ground. Looking down at the cup, Esteban braces himself as he then turns his attention to

Mario, who remains on the outside.

"Espera, no vienes?" Esteban asks as the helicopter continues to rise from the ground. As the sound of the motor starts to intensify, the bursting winds below causes Mario to back off a bit before returning his attention to Esteban.

"No me necesitan aqui hermaño," Mario replies as he waves farewell when Roxanne pokes her head out from the shadows.

"Mi amor volvere," Roxanne replies as she leans back as Esteban salutes Diego as the helicopter reaches a high enough point. As Mario stands in salute, the helicopter takes off over the sea as he drops his hand. Following it as he goes over the water, he watches as it makes its way in the trail of its wake.

Now with his eyes focusing on the vast plain of water, Esteban takes a couple of sips from the cup. Feeling the caffeine and sugar's effects flow through his veins, he searches for any trace of the boat and the wake it leaves behind. As the blue plasters itself all through the horizon, shreds of remnant foam start to appear. Coming closer to the horizon, the boat appears as it rocks with the choppy waters. Feeling the intensity of the flames swell from his core, he tightens his grasp around the rope that hangs just short of the doorframe. As the sounds of the motor fade as he focuses in on the boat, Esteban examines the decks in search of his son when a hand lands down on his shoulder.

"Esta es tu pelea," Roxanne says as it breaks the monotonous repetition of the swinging blades above their heads.

Turning his attention back to the approaching boat, Esteban then shifts his focus on her once again before looking on in confusion.

"Por que?" Esteban asks as Roxanne turns her attention forward to the soldiers inside the cockpit.

Before she can reply, the radio in the center console starts to buzz and vibrate causing the pilot to shift the channels. As the noise fades into silence suddenly a voice starts to speak.

"Si tienes preguntas llama cinco tres-." The voice says swiftly before dissipating into static. As it fades, the pilot turns to Esteban and Roxanne in the back as they continue to look in confusion.

"Sigue cambiando de estacion," Roxanne yells as the pilot turns the dial more when another voice starts to ring out.

"Helicoptero no identificado, este es el guardacostas, regresa ahora," the voice says before cutting out. Once more the pilot turns back except this time with a far more serious tone in his face. He then watches as Roxanne turns to Esteban before they both turn their attentions back to the pilot as he keeps his hands on the wheel.

"Esta es tu parada," the pilot says as he starts to turn the helicopter to the left a little bit. As it hangs over the airspace above the boat, it remains still as Esteban turns to Roxanne as he remains back in her chair.

"Gracias por el subidon de energía," Esteban says as he lifts the cup into the air before toasting to her. Before she can reply, he then chugs down the remaining liquid as he feels the bitter chunks of energy flow through his body. As the flames start to enter his eyes, he turns toward the opening along the side before shifting himself.

"Dejame darte esto antes de que te vayas," Roxanne says as it turns Esteban's attention to her. As he watches on, she reaches into her jacket and suddenly pulls out a red apple. A couple of bruises from the travel, she gives it to him as he looks down in confusion.

"Para que es esto?" Esteban asks as his hand wraps around the apple before placing it inside one of his pockets.

"Para que tu loco hermaño manzana pueda ayudarte desde lejos," Roxanne replies as Esteban smirks before nodding his head.

"Esta bien, ve y trata de no hacer demasiado ruido," the pilot says as he momentarily turns their attention before Esteban shifts back to the boat as it continues to sway in the water. With one final nod, the flames glow within the depths of his irises as he dives out of the helicopter as he aims for the boat. Cutting it close, he splashes down a couple feet from the back of the boat when suddenly he rises from the depths. Looking up to see the helicopter turning back as it heads back to Cuba, he turns his attention to the pristine white surface of the yacht. As the droplets of water slide down, Esteban turns to the ladder feet from him as he swims his way closer. Placing a hand on each railing, he prepares himself to lift from the water when suddenly something below his feet disturbs the water around him.

As his eyes open wider, he looks down at the surface to see small swells as vibrations start to echo about. Taking in the deepest breath he can, he drops his head below the surface of water. Then as he reopens his eyes, beyond the overwhelming pressure of the ocean a long shadow made of metal and bolts sits beneath the yacht. Keeping it upward, the motor beneath it keeps going at a slow yet steady rate when Esteban looks upward at the yacht. Feeling the pressure within his chest as the power of the breath starts to weaken, Esteban lifts back up as he exhales. Struggling to keep himself afloat, his hands tighten around the railing when his foot finds the bottom rung.

CHAPTER 15

Once it was steady, Esteban lifts himself out of the water as it falls back to the surface. Placing his first foot on the yacht, the other one follows with little hesitation as he takes a couple of steps toward the main cabin. Pausing for a moment, he locates a door a few steps away when he looks back at the sky. Seeing no trace of the helicopter, Esteban looks around before turning his attention to the door. With a turn of the bronze knob, he twists it free from the frame before pushing it open. Once the light starts to invade the darkness within, he steps inside to see the largest section of the yacht. A massive room awaits him as he continues inward as the bland, white walls surround him. Empty of any trace of any furnishing along the walls, Esteban continues further as he starts to hear the echo from the waves crashing against the hull. Inspecting his surroundings in silence, he makes his way toward the opposite end of the room where another door meets him.

Attempting to turn the knob, suddenly the sounds of whispers followed by laughter caught his attention. As his eyes dart around the area, he momentarily places his ear up against the body of the door. Hearing no difference, he then pulls his head back before twisting the doorknob. Opening the door to his surprise, he looks on as before him is a spiraling staircase which leads upward. Hearing the echoing of laughter outside of the chamber, he starts to make his way upward as he approaches the first door. Hearing the voices get louder, he continues around the stairs when he reaches the very top where another door awaits him. This time the voices grow dull as he opens the door wide to reveal the sunlight waiting for him on the outside.

Stepping into the Atlantic waters, Esteban follows the balcony around as his eyes adjust to the sun. Once they settle down, he turns his attention to find the source of the voices just in time for them to raise in volume. Cautiously leaning his head toward the railing, his eyes catch sight of a smaller yet more agile boat as it rocks along the side of the yacht. A fading orange color going around the hull from front to back, the boat bounces as the patriotic flag flaps along the white cabin. Before Esteban can take another step, he spots a Coast Guardsman standing in front of the railing with a dark blue shirt under a bright orange life vest. Blood dripping from his face as the bruises start to welt up, the man's chest struggles to take in a deep breath. Constricting his chest, the man pulls on the Velcro of the vest as he continues to look toward the hull.

Taking another step, Esteban starts to hear laughter as he places his hands along the guardrail. As the metal twists and tighten, he leans over to see Col. Lins and a group of four guards as they stand with guns drawn. As a smirk grows along his face, Col. Lins steps forward and lifts his hand up, causing the others to lower their weapons. After taking a pair of steps in both directions, the coast guardsman watches in fear as the soldiers keep their fingers on the triggers of the weapons. Then before long, Col. Lins stops in the middle as he turns his back on the man. Before speaking a word, he reaches down and pulls out a maroon flask before popping it open. A pair of swigs later, he wipes the brown fluid from his mouth before scanning over the bunch.

"Eres americaño?" Col. Lins asks as he looks over his shoulder at the man who continues to gaze over the group before him.

"Yes, I am a member of the U.S Coast Guard," the man says as he tries to regain some of his confidence.

"Lo que dice?" the soldiers ask amongst themselves as they turn to Col. Lins who smirks in response.

Turning around, Col. Lins extends his arm and tilts the canteen over as the brownish liquid within pours out into a foamy puddle. Once the last few drops pour out, he then turns to the man who shifts his attention back to Col. Lins.

"Lastima que esta bebida espumosa sea lo mejor que viene de tu país," Col. Lins says as his smirk fades. Keeping his attention on the man as the puddle starts to evaporate under the Caribbean sun, the man starts to look in confusion.

"Perdonen mi Español pero solo se un par de cosas," the man replies, impressing the soldiers behind Col. Lins as they turn their attention back to him.

Uncaring in his response, he momentarily looks over at the man before reaching to his side. Pulling out his pistol, he turns his focus on the man as he backs away at the sight of the gun. Lifting his hands to the sky as tears start to drop, the man starts to cower as Col. Lins starts to aim the gun. Then without a word, he fires off a pair of shots into the man, sending him stumbling back as he falls over the edge. Falling flat onto the boat beyond the yacht, Col. Lins charges forward as the rest of the soldiers stand by his side, looking in awe as the man's blood starts to mix with the water from the circling waves.

Meanwhile back above the top balcony, Esteban's rage starts to overtake him. Flames reverberating through his skeleton as the glow builds in his pupils, his hands tighten around the metal guardrails. As the metal starts to melt and disintegrate, he starts to clench his teeth as he watches Col. Lins toss his canteen over the railing before looking back at the rest of the group.

"Donde esta mi proximo suministro de cafeína?" Col. Lins asks as Esteban backs off before looking down at the broken shards of the metal railing. Looking at one another, the soldiers shrug their shoulders before turning back to Col. Lins who starts to grow angrier by the second. His face becoming as red as their national flag, he watches as one of the soldier leans in before whispering into another's ears. After a couple of seconds, the soldier stands straight as the other steps forward.

"Dile," the other soldier mumbles as the other looks on in hesitance before turning his attention to Col. Lins.

"Si soldado, hable por el grupo," Col. Lins replies as he starts to ball up his hands into fists.

"Has cambiado desde que encontraste esa adicción a la cafeína," the soldier replies as Col. Lins's hand falls flat before his jaw falls agape. Then after another moment, he keeps his focus on the soldier when he suddenly motions him forward. Seeing the hesitation in his eyes, he nods his head before taking a couple of steps closer to the man.

"Lo siento, tienes razon, no se lo que me has pasado," Col. Lins says as he once more tries to motion the man forward. After watching him take a couple of steps cautiously toward him, Col. Lins charges and wraps his arms around the man before giving him a hug.

"Lo se, coronel, solo queremos al hombre que respetamos de vuelta," the soldier says as Col. Lins stares at the other soldiers who attempt to avoid eye contact.

"Lo siento si rompi algo bueno," Col. Lins replies as he starts to smirk.

"Esta bien," the soldier replies as he keeps his sight on the moving clouds beyond the boats railing. Then after a moment or two of silence, another gunshot rings out which causes the other soldiers to step back against the hull of the boat.

Col. Lins step back as he drops the pistol on the floor as the soldier slumps onto the ground. Looking down at the man struggling to breath, he lifts him up before placing him up against the guard rail. As the two look on in silence, the rest of the group watches on in as blood streams down his thigh and leg. Dripping onto his foot as his color fades with each passing second, the man struggles to live as Col. Lins places his hand on the man's head. Then with little force he tilts the man's head down and points at the Coast Guard's corpse laying in a pool of blood.

"DONDE ESTA MI HIJO?" Esteban screams from the railing as

steam starts to pulsate from his pores. Their attention shifts toward him as he rips the remainder of the railing in half. Watching as the sections fall helplessly into the ocean, the line of soldiers aim their weapons as Col. Lins turns around.

With a smile on his face, Col. Lins turns to the fading soldier at his side before shifting his sight back to Esteban who steps toward the edge.

"Podria esta ren cualquiera de estos barcos o no," Col. Lins replies with a chuckle as Esteban grows angrier by the second. As the flames spread through his limbs, his mouth falls agape when suddenly he releases a fireball. Watching as it spins in their direction, the soldiers duck down when Col. Lins grabs hold of the man and places him in front of himself. Making impact with the two, they fly before crashing down onto the broken body of the Coast Guardsman. Shards of metal and embers raining throughout, the fragments start to liter the surface of the water. Unable to believe the transpiring events, the line of soldiers turn back to the remains of the two men when suddenly Col. Lins pushes the burnt corpse of the soldier off him. Without a scratch he rises to his feet as Esteban remains behind them as he regains his composure.

Seeing his status, the group turns back to Esteban before drawing their guns as they take aim. Then as silence starts to settle on the scene, the engine of the boat below starts to rev as it turns their attention once more.

"Mata a ese fraude," Col. Lins proclaims as he grabs the wheel before turning the boat around in the wreckage of broken metal. With his command sent, the soldiers turn back to Esteban as he continues to watch their fingers approach their respective triggers. Then one by one their guns fire bullets through the humid air, taking their trajectory toward Esteban when he flies up and over them. Attempting to take another try, Esteban grabs hold of two soldiers as he then throws them off the boat. Splashing down into the water, Esteban lands on the deck just feet from the rest of the soldiers. Before any can make another move, an alarm sounds off as suddenly the sound of charging footsteps make their way around the boat. Getting closer, the soldiers keep their guns drawn as they take a step back. Then one by one they turn their attention to the left where a shadow approaches from the staircase.

As they continue to look, Esteban watches as with each second the soldier who took his son hostage earlier reappears. Stopping after stepping off the final step, the soldier snarls as he sees Esteban when the other soldiers start to look at their weapons.

"Dirigete al submarine y dejaños," the soldier says as he starts to unbutton his camo jacket. Once the final button frees itself, he then throws the jacket off the boat before turning his attention to the soldiers who nod in unison. One by one they place their weapons back into their holsters when they swiftly make their way past him and down the stairs. As the last one disappears, the soldier steps forward as he starts to crack the bones in his hands as the muscles flex up his arms. Identifying him as the one who took his son, the burning flames reignite as he takes a step forward. Facing off with one another, door slamming beneath them shifts their attention momentarily.

Before Esteban can bring it back, the soldier charges forward and slams him into the metal railing. Denting the surface, the soldier backs away as Esteban grimaces before the soldier smirks when he delivers a punch across Esteban's face. Turning him about, Esteban grabs ahold of the top railing before flames start to ignite the darkness within his pupils. Then with a primordial scream, Esteban rips the top bar off the railing. Hearing the soldier's footsteps as they get closer, Esteban turns around and slams the bar across his head. Stunning the man, he stumbles about as Esteban attempts to deliver another blow. Getting within inches of the man's skull, he drops down as the bar smacks into the side of the boat. Clanging about the space, the soldier slams his fist into Esteban's back and ribs before delivering a couple more.

With each blow, Esteban's anger continues to intensify as the soldier delivers another blow. Sending him into the side of the boat, his body quivers with the impact as he grimaces before looking over at the soldier. Turning his back on Esteban, the soldier raises his arms in celebration before stopping in his place. Without moving, he turns his attention over his shoulder to see as Esteban tries to shake off the pain as he spits out a glob of blood and saliva. Snarling, he then turns around before charging up as he delivers a haymaker that strikes him across Esteban's jaw. Causing him to crumble, Esteban's arms shake as he attempts to get himself back to his feet.

"Solo quedate y muere," the soldier says as he continues to watch as Esteban's arms fully extend.

As Esteban attempts to get back to his feet, the soldier chops him down with a swift kick to his ribs. With the impact, flames spurt from Esteban's mouth as steam begins to release from his nostrils. Suddenly, his arms get weak as he falls flat against the floor.

The soldier then snickers as he turns his attention to the stairway leading to the bottom floor. Shaking his head, he makes his way toward the top stair when he places his hand on top of the railing. After a moment of the railing clanging, the soldier places his foot down on the top step before lifting his other.

Meanwhile behind him, Esteban's eyes reopen as his hands tighten into fists. Picking himself up, he looks over at the soldier who continues to make his way down the stairs.

"Eso es lo gracioso de las tormentas," Esteban mutters as he gets back to his feet. Watching as the soldier stops himself along the third step, he pounds his hand down on the railing.

"Que es eso?" the soldier asks as he keeps his focus on the remainder of the stairwell ahead of him.

"Despues de la calma del centro, la fuerza se libera," Esteban replies as he starts to shake. Then before the soldier can look back, Esteban charges forward as he then tackles the man causing them to tumble down the stairs. Grimacing with each hit, the two men finally roll onto the deck of the bottom level. First to his feet, Esteban cracks his neck before brushing off the thin layer of sand along the wooden panels. As he watches, the soldier starts to chuckle as he gets back to his feet revealing the streak of blood falling from between his lips.

"Tu dedicacion a tu país y tu familia es tu debilidad," the soldier says as he uses his wrist to wipe the blood clear.

"No te preocupes, encontrare a mi hijo sin importar donde este en este yate," Esteban replies as the soldier starts to smile as he reveals the blood covering his teeth.

"Estas tan ciego para var que esta pelea no es más que una distracción," the soldier says as he looks out to the wáter. With his attention turning, whistles break the sea breeze as Esteban charges over to the broken handrail. Catching sight of the submarine as he sits atop of the churning waters, the top hatch opens to the elements as two men stand behind another. Upon further inspection, Esteban's eyes widen as he sees his son in front of the men with bruises all over his face. On his knees, one of the men behind him, walks around him carefully to not fall off when he starts to pull out his gun. Firmly in his grasp, the man places it against the side of Rafael's head. Tears flowing down his eyes, Rafael looks down at the silverish metal beneath him.

"Como dije que tun debilidad te destrozara," the soldier says from behind Esteban.

"Lo dejo ir," Esteban yells as he watches the soldier to Rafael's side place his finger on the trigger.

"Dejame pensar en ello," the soldier replies as he places his bulky arm along Esteban's shoulders. Looking over at the man's draping hand as it lays aimlessly along the air, Esteban then turns his attention to the man's smirking face.

"Que es la palabra?" the gun toting soldier asks as his finger gets closer to the trigger.

"Llevalo al Col. Lins," the soldier replies as the man lifts the gun upwards and fires the one in the chamber into the sky. As the realization hits Esteban, he watches as the man places the gun back into its holster as they turn their attention back to Rafael. As they begin to pick him back up, Esteban turns to the soldier behind him. Before he can make a move, the man grabs hold of Esteban's head and slams it into one of the windows behind them. With glass exploding in all directions, the soldier pulls Esteban back before crashing him back into the wall.

Struggling to keep his breath, Esteban looks back as he watches the soldier head over to the railing as he points his hand out to sea. As he struggles to get himself free, the sounds of the submarine's engine roaring dwell down as it drops beneath the ocean surface. Trails of blood making their way down to his chin, Esteban balls up his hands before charging at the soldier once more. This time before he can prepare up a defense, Esteban uses some of his strength to deliver a combo of strikes. As his head bounces from left to right, Esteban delivers a flurry of shots to his sides causing the man to struggle to reflect as much as he can. However to little avail, Esteban continues his assault with one last haymaker that connects across the soldier's jaw.

CHAPTER 16

Spinning the man, he slams into the railing when Esteban lifts him over as he struggles to hang on by a fingernail. Swaying along the edge, he tries to pull himself up as Esteban takes a couple of steps away. After a couple of failures, he then tries to keep his grasp as his sight turns to Esteban.

"No puedes dejarme aqui," the soldier screams as Esteban turns his attention back to him.,

"Donde esta Col. Lins?" Esteban asks as he gets closer to the soldier who once again tries to pull himself up.

"La parte de América más cercaña a tu hogar," the soldier yells as he continues to hang on. Before Esteban makes the next move, the soldier loses his grasp, starting to fall toward the ocean. Just as his hands start to flail just below the deck, Esteban sprints over and reaches down to grab him by the wrist. With his fingers wrapping around the man's arm, Esteban lifts him back up as he hangs over the railing. Recovering his breath as he looks down at the waves that continue to crash back and forth.

"Ayudame a llegar a el," Esteban says as he extends his hand to the man. Watching as one of his hands fall as he tries to brace himself; the man looks at Esteban in relief before once again turning toward the flailing ocean.

"No puedo," the soldier replies as he looks back at Esteban.

"Por qué?" Esteban asks as he looks over at the man who then places his hand on top of the handrail.

"Eres un falso heroe Cubano," the soldier says as he launches a glob of saliva in Esteban's face. Chuckling hysterically, he watches as Esteban turns his head before wiping the remnants from his cheek. As his laughter swims through his ears, the rage within Esteban ignites as the flames restore themselves within his eyes. However, before Esteban can turn his attention back, the soldier pulls out a knife from beneath his belt and slams it down into Esteban's hand. The clanging of the metal tip hitting the guardrail, pain and horror shivers up Esteban's arm as he looks at the soldier. Continuing to laugh, he then pulls the blade out before Esteban can make another move. Once it was free, the soldier turns the blade onto himself before attempting to stab himself in the abdomen.

However, before the blade can pierce his skin, Esteban reaches over and grabs hold of the hilt as blood from his hand turns the black leather red. His eyes widening in shock, the soldier watches as Esteban rips the blade free before sending it down toward the depths of the ocean below. Carelessly, the soldier struggles to hang on with one hand as his other flails behind him. Struggling to keep his balance, Esteban grabs the soldier's arm and yanks him forward. As his frame sits parallel with the handrail, Esteban stares into his eyes as the flames spin through his corneas.

"Fui un heroe una vez, pero ahora soy mas," Esteban says as he grabs the man by the collar of his army jacket.

"Que seria eso? Un fracaso?" the soldier replies as he completely lets go of the rail while he tries to break free from Esteban's hold.

"No yo soy el latido de la madre Cuba," Esteban replies as the flames fill up his eyes as he shifts his attention. Placing it on his bleeding hand, they watch as the wound seals up on its own. Once the mark is gone, Esteban returns his sight to the fearful soldier as he attempts to break free. Then before the soldier can make another move, suddenly the sounds of vibrations turn their attention upwards. To their surprise, the two men see a hovering helicopter as a rope ladder drops down. Starting to hang just feet from his shadow, he watches a man poke his head out from the back door. Smirking at the sight of the familiar face, he then starts to let the soldier go when he starts to flail.

Struggling to hold himself, the soldier catches a finger on the metal bar as Esteban backs away from him. Growing closer to the ladder, the soldier pulls himself closer to the boat as Esteban keeps his focus on the helicopter above.

"Tu hijo se va a morir," the soldier says as he shifts Esteban's attention as he clenches his teeth. Watching him get closer, the soldier looks down at the crashing waves before turning his attention back to Esteban. Stopping just feet from the dangling man, Esteban then reaches into his pocket and pulls out the apple that Roxanne gave him earlier.

"No cuando tengo a Cuba detrás de mi," Esteban replies as he turns his attention to the soldier. Before he can reply, Esteban swings the apple across the soldier's face. Exploding into pulp upon impact, the color in the man's face fades as his strength dissipates. Releasing his hold on the metal, the soldier falls into the churning waters before disappearing below the surface. Meanwhile, wiping the pulp from his hand, he looks down at the foamy surface seeing nothing. Shifting his attention back to the rope ladder, Esteban starts to make his way to the top as once more he sees the man's head poking out.

"Le pegaste con una manzana," the man says as he watches Esteban climb rung after rung.

"Si bien mi amigo hubiera hecho lo mismo," Esteban replies as his hand about reaches the final rung that hangs just shy of the opening to the helicopter. The pilot pulling his head back, Esteban lifts himself as he watches the man head back into the cockpit. With his hands back on the console, Esteban watches as the man turns back to him.

"Hacia donde nos dirigimos?" the man asks as he watches Esteban turn his attention toward the horizon. Suddenly his sight catches a glimpse of the speeding submarine as it flows through the depths of the ocean.

"De esa manera," Esteban replies as he points toward the windshield. With a nod, the man pulls up on a lever as the blades above their heads start to increase their spin. Taking a seat along the back, Esteban watches as the helicopter starts to fly through the crimson sky. The sun sliding into the ocean, the men watch as they head through the air when the pilot looks back.

"Por que no volaste?" the pilot asks as it turns Esteban's attention.

"Tratando de ahorrar mi energia para el rescate por delante," Esteban replies as he looks at his hands. Feeling a tingling chorusing through his fingers, he turns back to the open air as they continue forward.

As the helicopter spins forward, they watch as land starts to approach along the edge of sight. Trying to decipher their location, they look all around when something behind them catches their attention.

Esteban then takes his forearm and removes some smudging as it starts to reveal some lettering along the metal. In white, the letters USCG become visible as he then turns back to the pilot behind him.

"Como obtuviste esto?" Esteban asks as the pilot looks over his shoulder.

"Lo encontre en Col. Lins escondite secreto después de dejar a tu amiga," the pilot replies before returning his attention forward.

"Como lo conseguiste sobre el espacio aéreo de América?" Esteban asks.

"Mate algo de inglés para convencerlos de que era estadounidense," the pilot replies with a smirk.

"Como lo aprendiste?" Esteban asks as he keeps his attention on the pilot.

"Escucharia la radio estadounidense que tenían que escuchar si no estaban tramando nada bueno," the pilot replies as he starts to nod his head as he keeps his hands steady.

"Que estas haciendo?" Esteban asks as the pilot stops before looking back at him once again.

"Recordando esta cancion que tocaron mucho," the pilot replies as he turns his attention back onto the skies.

Seeing the approaching landmass beneath them, Esteban returns to the opening along the side to get a better look. Placing his hand on the frame, he then pokes his head out when he sees the beach in front of them getting closer. As the visibility continues to weaken, Esteban looks around when suddenly something catches his attention. From a couple of miles away, he recognizes a large yellow landmark along the boardwalk. It was the circular object from the computer projection that he and Roxanne saw during their search of the base back in Cuba. Realizing what it was, Esteban points in its direction, causing the pilot to shift his flight. Making his way closer, the two men keep their eyes focusing when something rises from the shallowing waters.

Surprisingly, the object is none other than the submarine as they watch it approach the shoreline. Then as it gets within feet of the line, it sinks beneath the water before disappearing under the approaching night sky.

"Supongo que esta por ahí," the pilot says as he continues their trek toward the location.

"Estoy seguro de ello," Esteban replies before pointing to a large object sitting along the grains of sand. Growing closer, Esteban recognizes the boat that Col. Lins rode to his escape. Continuing to approach, the two men look around at the vacant landscape as they continue toward the section of rock and sand.

"Esta es tu parada," the pilot says as he looks back to see Esteban nod before turning his own attention back to the opening along the side. Just as he places his hand back along the frame, Esteban pauses before looking at the pilot who puts the helicopter into idle.

"Por cierto cual es tu nombre?" Esteban asks as the pilot turns his head.

"Mi nombre es Raul," the pilot replies before saluting Esteban who nods his head.

"Es possible que quieras quedarte si necesito un vuelo de regreso," Esteban says with a smirk before diving out of the helicopter when he directs his fall to the boat wreckage. Passing through the low cumulus clouds, flames start to spark up as embers shoot from the pores within his skin. Trailing downward, he lands down onto a knee beside the boat when he turns his attention toward the helicopter. Catching a brief glimpse of Raul's hand waving farewell, he watches as the helicopter turns off before disappearing into the darkening sky. With no trace of it left, Esteban turns his attention to the rocky side of the landscape. Examining each one for the easiest path upward, he stops suddenly when his foot lands on something clumpy. Looking down at the grains of sand, his eyes catch sight of a darker spot as he shifts his attention toward his hand. Then from within his fingerprints, flames start to light like kindle as it provides him with the necessary light.

Turning his attention back to the substance, he sees a large spot of dark red blood as it trails over to the cliff wall. Standing back to his feet, Esteban makes his way over to the wall using the glow from his hand to lead the way. Continuing to follow the droplets even as they get smaller, he stops himself at the edge of the boulder before him. Starting to progress up the wall, the flames along his hand snuff out as he places it beside the next level of blood drops. Continuing to make his way up the rocks as he keeps his focus on the beads of blood, Esteban struggles to keep his balance.

Then finally as he reaches the top, he pulls himself upward as the faint streetlights turn on around him. A few flicker as he turns his attention to the large circular landmark. With nothing but the buzzing lights and the gentle breeze surrounding him, Esteban stops himself at the foot of the object. Then between the sections of darkness, the glowing aura reveals a faint handprint as it sits on a word near the top. Seeing more of it, he watches as beneath a blood smear handprint is the word Cuba about five rows up.

Then with a deep breath, he places his hand on top of the word when he feels some give behind it. Then after a gentle push, the word caves in as suddenly the landmark starts to rumble and vibrate. Trembling the space around it, Esteban steps back when he watches a bright light split the entire object directly in the center. Once it gets to the bottom, he watches as it opens before him. Folding itself in half, Esteban watches as it reveals a large hole leading downward below the ground. Then just as he attempts to jump through, the darkness fills with a circular platform of cement. Once it is secure, Esteban steps on it as suddenly the platform slowly makes its way back down. Looking up at the night, he sees the landmark closing back up. Forcing himself to look around, his eyes widen as he starts to see his surroundings.

Closing in around him, chambers of metal and stone surround him even as they sit completely empty. With little furnishings, Esteban continues to search for any trace of Col. Lins when the platform beneath him comes to a stop. Bracing his legs for the shock, he then turns to the massive space around him when he steps off. Looking around at the faintly lit area, he passes through without provocation until finally reaching an open doorway. Just as he is about to step forward, his foot freezes in the air when a series of screams and chain rattling echo out. Once it fades, Esteban charges through the series of doorways when he comes face to face with a shut door and a bronze doorknob. Attempting to place his hand on the metal, the sound of faint voices string through the cracks of the door. Feeling the flames rising through his body, he turns the knob causing the door to creak open.

Revealing the room on the other end, Esteban steps through to see the large platform that sits around him. On the opposing end of the chamber, the massive submarine sits just a foot above the watery surface. Beside it, a group of soldiers stand around as in the center a man with chains around his hands stands along the back. With a large strip of fabric covering his eyes, the rest of the group talks amongst themselves when suddenly one of the men steps forward.

"Donde esta el coronel con nuestra paga?" the man asks as he looks around the bare room. As Esteban prepares to speak, suddenly a buzzing sound starts to echo throughout the room.

"Estoy cerca asi que cuida tu boca Osvaldo," Col. Lin's voice says as it clears through a shield of static. As his words reverberate around the room, the group of men look around in search of Col. Lins as the leader steps forward. His tall frame along with his tan skin brought him forward along with his hazel eyes and black hair.

"Por qué nos traido a este lugar?" Osvaldo asks as he continues to search for the source. After a couple of seconds, another round of buzzing sounds when it clears from the silence.

"No le faltes al respeto a mi tienda de dulces, de lo contrario sufriras las consecuencias," Col. Lins replies as suddenly the lights turn on in the room. Revealing inch by inch, the group of men watch as barrels of explosive reveal themselves with each section. Rope tying every square inch together, everyone's sight follows the rope toward an open doorway along the other side of the room. Heading into the darkness, they watch as a single flickering flame appears before heading out into the open space. Once into the light, the source reveals itself as a group of soldiers in heavy armor walk through the opening.

Coming together, they drop to a knee as they point their rifles at the opposing group as Esteban watches from the last few dark sections of the room. Hidden from view, he watches as the men load their weapons as the other group prepares their own. Then before a bullet is fired, one of the men pulls out a lighter and lights it. Bringing it closer to his face, everyone watches him smile as it reveals his teeth with golden canines. With each passing second the tension grows even as Osvaldo starts to smirk. Before it reaches laughter level, he stops before turning his attention to the kneeling Rafael.

"Pasamelo y luego podras escapar en tu pequeño submarino de metal," Osvaldo yells before smirking.

"No somos todos amigos aquí?" the soldier asks before looking at the guards' holding guns to Rafael's head.

With no response, Osvaldo looks back at his own group before starting to laugh. After a brief chuckle, he then turns back to the other group before looking around the room.

"Algunos de nosotros somos enemigos, tal vez incluso traidores," Osvaldo replies before snapping his fingers. Before anyone else can speak or move, a single gunshot fires off as one of the men behind the soldier crumbles to the floor. As the rest look back as blood starts to slither down his face, the men in front of them remain with their guns steady. Even as a single shell falls to the ground, the soldiers turn their attention back to the others, angrier than before.

"Entregarlo u otro morira," Col. Lins's voice chimes in from the speakers as the group of soldiers look toward each other. Then in unison they gulp down before a pair lifts Rafael back to his feet. As the two guards start to push him forward, Esteban continues to look on from the shadows.

Before he can lift his foot, Osvaldo takes a couple of steps toward the approaching Rafael. Once he is in his reach, he then grabs hold of Rafael's shoulder and pulls him closer. As the soldier looks on curiously, Osvaldo shoves Rafael onto his knees as he starts to cower in fear.

"Vamos Cubano cobarde," Osvaldo yells when he reaches back and pulls out his pistol. Placing it on Rafael's temple, he then looks around as Rafael struggles to hold back his tears. Sliding down his face, Osvaldo and his group of militants look around to no answer. His emotion souring, he then pulls the gun away before hitting Rafael across the face with the blunt end. As Rafael falls onto his face, Osvaldo shakes his head before kneeling at his side. Then as Rafael struggles to get to his knees, Osvaldo pulls him up by the shirt as once more Rafael kneels before him. Placing the gun once more, his finger slides beside the trigger as he looks around once more.

"Esa es una gran charla para alguien que golpea a un hombre con las maños detrás de la espalda," Esteban says as he steps from the shadows. Flames swallowing his corneas as it snakes its way around his body, he steps into the light as a glow starts to brighten the area around him. Watching as Osvaldo clicks down the safety, Esteban continues forward when suddenly another round of static rings out.

"Bueno, ahora que estas aquí, no necesito de ti," Col. Lins says as he coughs just before the intercom shuts off. Then as the group of soldiers beside the submarine look at one another, suddenly gunshots start to ring out as one by one they drop lifeless along with Osvaldo. Each one bleeding from various spots as their bodies fall helplessly into the water, the other group watches on even as Esteban turns his attention to his son. As he starts to open his mouth, the man in front of the group starts to smile as his golden teeth shine for all to see.

"Ellos no eran dignos de ser parte de nuestro reino," the man says as the rest of the group turn their guns toward Esteban. As they get into place, the man then makes his way once more beside Rafael.

Shifting his direction, the man then lifts the blindfold so Rafael and Esteban can see each other. However after a couple of seconds, the man picks him up before shoving him into a couple of guards. Once there, the men grab him by the shoulders as they start to make their way toward the open doorway. Continuing the approach, the man turns to Esteban as the flames start to filter down his limbs as the anger starts to intensify. Then as a fireball starts to leach out from the pores within his hands, the man turns the gun to Esteban who stops momentarily before starting to chuckle. Steam and embers escaping between every breath, Esteban turns his attention onto the man.

"Tus balas no pueden hacerme nada," Esteban says as spurts of flames shoot out.

CHAPTER 17

Placing his finger back along the trigger, one of the soldiers beside the submarine lets out a groan, shifting their attention. Not for long though as the man fires off a shot into the soldier's body silencing the sounds. Turning his attention back, the man returns the focus to Esteban who looks over at the dimly light doorway. Hearing the remaining militants behind him load their weapon as well, Esteban turns back when suddenly another round of static noise chimes into the room.

"Oficial, dejemelo a mi, pero por favor deshágase de los cadáveres," Col Lins says as the man snarls as his attention shifts toward the intercom above them. Once the sound was off, the man turns his focus back onto Esteban before shaking his head at the request as his finger gets closer to the trigger. As the others lower their weapons and start to head over to the bloody bodies, one of the men stops as he then turns toward the man.

"Es major hacer lo que dice, sabes lo que la paso a la ultima persona que lo enojo," the militant says as the other one stops just shy of the bodies. Meanwhile ignoring the words of the militant, the man keeps the gun pointing at Esteban, shaking it as he struggles to decide. Before he can get the gun down, another round of static choruses into the room as the other militants turn their attention upwards.

"Mejor date prisa, la confiteria empieza a olar a muerte," Col. Lins chimes in as the intercom shuts off before anyone can reply. Then with a deep breath, the man lowers the gun before turning his attention to the others as they continue to make their way over to the broken bodies that liter the floor. One by one, they start to toss the bodies into the murky waters around the submarine as Esteban turns his attention toward the open doorway. Taking a charge as he gets closer, he proceeds toward the opening when suddenly he stops to take in what awaits him. After a series of thunderous splashes ceases, whistling forces Esteban's attention back to the men behind him.

"No te me escapas Tormenta Cubano," the man says as he once more points his gun directly at Esteban, who remains frozen in the doorway.

"Haz lo que hay que hacer," Col. Lins voice mutters inside the room as the man smiles to show his teeth.

"Finalmente algo con lo que los Cubanos podemos estar de acuerdo," the man replies as his finger approaches the trigger. Then just as he goes to pull it, another shot rings out causing Esteban to turn his head. However, to his surprise, he feels no sting - instead he watches as the man falls to the ground in a puddle of blood. Life fading, the man struggles to breathe as suddenly the militant beside him shrugs his shoulders before kicking him into the water just over the edge. Gone from sight as his eyes fade to white, the militants put away their guns before heading over to the ramp leading to the submarine. Once they are in place, they place their hands behind their back as Esteban continues to watch on. Turning his attention, Esteban looks back at the open hall before him as another doorway awaits him.

With each step closer, the sounds of rattling chains echo throughout as Esteban clears his sight into the main room. In front of him lay a vast space of barrels and crates as before him his son stands helpless inside of a cage. Seeing his son within range, the flames and anger that drive him fade as he starts to rush over to him. However, before he can get any closer, he stops in his tracks as the chains start to rattle as a pair of machetes grind against them. On the end of their handles, Col. Lins steps into the light with a massive Cuban cigar between his lips.

Taking in a deep inhalation, he then takes out the cigar before releasing a bellowing smoke that spirals toward the ceiling. As he taps the cigar against the machete, tobacco falls along with ash onto the floor when he flicks it to the side. As it spins through the air, Col. Lins places another machete into his other hand as the rusty blades take aim against Esteban.

"No te preocupes hijo, serás libre pronto," Esteban says as Col. Lins chuckles as he looks back at Rafael who steps back in the cage.

"Ayudame papa," Rafael cries out before silencing as Col. Lins places the edge of the blades up against the cage.

"No romper este momento, pero tu muerte se debe," Col. Lins says before turning his attention to Esteban as flames start to chimney up his sternum. Shifting the blades to Esteban, Col. Lins screams as he charges forth with the machete swinging around. Preparing for the attack, the flames spread into Esteban's arms as once more steam starts to release from his pores. With every strike attempt, Esteban dodges the brunt of it before another one can make its way around. Screaming between strikes, one last blow misses when suddenly Col. Lins delivers a straight kick to Esteban's chest. The impact vibrating the center of his ribcage, Esteban takes a step back before sliding to a stop.

Nostrils flaring, the flames inside of him make their way up into his throat as suddenly the base of his throat starts to glow. Then as smoke escapes from between his lips, he starts to open his mouth when Col. Lins steps aside to place Rafael in the line of fire.

"Sueltalo, te reto," Col. Lins says with a smirk as he points the machetes towards Rafael. As his words reverberate, the flames extinguish as he relaxes his muscles, staring heavily into Rafael's face. Tears flowing down his face, Esteban's attention shifts as the sounds of Col. Lins' laughter breaks up the moment.

"Pelea conmigo de hombre a hombre," Esteban replies as the flames sink down his chest. For a moment, the laughter stops when Col. Lins points the blades back at Esteban.

"Excepto que eres mas que un hombre promedio," Col. Lins replies as he starts to cough. Dropping the machetes onto the floor, he places his hand over his mouth before staring at Esteban with his face reddening after each fit. Then as it stops, he lowers his hand to reveal the grin hiding beneath it. Before Esteban can reply, Col. Lins turns his attention toward a barrel that sits beside Rafael's cage. Just as he turns around, he picks up one of the machetes and makes his way to the barrel. Then as Esteban continues to look on, Col. Lins looks over at the machete before switching his focus to the wooden lid in front of him. Then as Col. Lins looks up, he uses the handle of the machete to smash open the barrel as spurts of liquid fall to the ground.

"Que estas haciendo?" Esteban asks as he watches as Rafael looks over at the open barrel.

"Voy a romper tu poder de fuego," Col. Lins replies before dunking his head inside the barrel as a wave of brown liquid falls into a puddle. Foaming at the surface, he then picks his head up before wiping his face clean of any remnants.

"El es como tu," Rafael yells as Col. Lins slams the machete into the chains of the cage before turning his attention to Esteban. Then before anyone can say a word, Col. Lins grabs the edge of the lip with his hand and tips it over as the brown liquid gushes toward Esteban. Making its way closer, it crashes into his ankles as it then makes its way past him.

"Tal desperdicio de una fuente de energía," Col. Lins replies as he looks at his body as his muscles start to strain even as his frame starts to grow. Catching his sight, Col. Lins kneels and grabs the other machete just before it can float away.

Watching as the veins in his neck swell, Esteban takes a step back as Col. Lins places the handles of the machetes together before looking at Esteban who continues to look on.

"Que has hecho?" Esteban asks.

"Me dije a mi mismo que ya no seria mas débil que un granjero," Col. Lins replies as he snarls, causing Rafael to retreat into the cage.

"De que estas hablando?" Esteban asks as Col. Lins reaches into his pocket and pulls out a vial as his other hand holds both machetes. As Esteban watches on, Col. Lins pops the cork out with his mouth and then spits it out into the accessible area of the room. Once it was clear, the reddish fluid inside starts to sway as Col. Lins turns his focus back to Esteban.

"Tu sangre es la clave para aprovechar esta fuerza," Col. Lins replies as he swallows down the liquid before Esteban can reply. Once the final drop is down into his stomach, Col. Lins throws the vial into the darkness as he then turns his attention to the machetes in his other hand.

"No puedes manejar el poder que viene con esa mezcla," Esteban says as he continues to watch as Col. Lins plays around with the set of machetes.

"No te preocupes, mi equipo ha pasado años perfeccionando tu sangre cubana en el potencial de poder perfecto," Col. Lins replies as he cracks his neck and fingers.

"Me interpondré en tu camino para no lastimar a nadie mas," Esteban replies as once more flames start to take hold within his corneas.

"Como cuando ni siquiera puedes soportar los vientos de una verdadera tormenta," Col. Lins says as he turns his attention to Esteban. Placing the machetes handle to handle, he smirks when he starts to spin them in a circle faster with each passing second. With each ensuing moment, the winds from the movement pick up causing Esteban to drift back to his surprise. Seeing his feet slide, Col. Lins speeds up as with one mighty spin Esteban crashes into a set of barrels.

Grimacing as he gets up, Esteban looks back to see the indentation from his body within the center of the barrel. As brown fluid starts to stream out from holes within the wood, Esteban reaches down before placing his finger at the source. Once it was coated, he places it inside of his mouth as he tastes the sweet liquid as he turns his attention to Col. Lins.

"Esta no es café Cubano," Esteban says as his focus switches only to find no one beyond Rafael. As the sound of his words go mute, he takes a couple of steps forward even as his eyes dart around. Continuing to observe the room, the sound of his own footprints echo about as Rafael steps toward the cage door. Then as he goes to take another step, he freezes like a deer when a set of headlights crack through the darkness. Before long an engine rumbles as lights start to get larger. Preparing for his defense, Esteban listens as the engine growls when it makes its approach. Coming toward him, the flames within his body spread upwards as he prepares a counter. Then as it reaches his throat, Esteban spits fire as it makes its way toward the approaching vehicle.

Revealing the body of the Humvee as they fly past, the streaks of light slam into the wall behind it. Even as a pair strikes the windshield, the Humvee continues closer as it speeds up. Then before he can spit another, the Humvee strikes Esteban as it sends him rolling up on the hood. As the brakes screech to a halt, Esteban falls back down as he lands with a thud. Remaining still along the ground, his nostrils flare as the smell of the exhaust spreads throughout the space. Even as he struggles to get back to life, the driver's door opens as Col. Lin steps out before making his way around the vehicle.

Once at Esteban's side, Col. Lins kicks him over onto his back before grabbing hold of his torn shirt collar. Firmly in his grasp, Col. Lins lifts him up before slamming him down onto the hood of the Humvee.

"Realmente pensaste que la investigación se detuvo hace tanto tiempo?" Col. Lins asks as Esteban groans with arms spread out. Still struggling to move, Col. Lins makes his way over to the driver's side door. Leaning inside, he disappears momentarily before revealing a machete back within his grasp. Smiling from ear to ear, he then makes his way over to the prone body of Esteban before shifting his gaze over to the rusty machete.

"Siempre tuve la esperanza," Esteban grumbles as his chest steadily rises and falls.

"Entonces que mueras con la piedad de toda una isla," Col. Lins chuckles as he turns his attention toward Esteban. Then as he remains prone on the hood, Col. Lins unleashes a downward swing of the machete toward him. However, as it gets closer, Esteban punches out the broken windshield and falls into the cab of the Humvee. The machete slamming through the hood, it slices through with ease as Col. Lins steams at the sight. Leaving the blade within the layers of engine parts, he then makes his way back over to the driver's door. Ripping it from the hinges, Col. Lins tosses it aside as he peers inside the cab. Before his head can make it through, Esteban slings a blade across Col. Lins's face. Blood sliding across his face, his hand goes over it before coming back down to eye level. Coating the skin, blood turns his hand red as Col. Lins steps back.

Allowing him space to get out, Esteban slithers out of the cab before attempting to deliver another attack. As the blade gets within inches, Col. Lins punches it out of the air as it cracks loose from the handle.

Sliding across the stone ground, Col. Lins turns his attention to Esteban as he wraps his hand around his neck. Firmly in his grasp, he lifts Esteban within a hair length as he snarls in his face. Then as his bloody eyes stare into Esteban's soul, the wound miraculously heals on its own as his tan skin returns without a blemish.

"Estas fuera de tu liga," Col. Lins yells in his face before delivering a haymaker to the side of Esteban's face. Watching him crumble to the ground, Col. Lins chuckles as Esteban struggles back to his feet.

Esteban gets to his feet as the flames continue to build with the rage inside of his body. Reaching his fingertips, smoke starts to release from his nostrils as he turns his attention to Col. Lins.

"He estado hacienda esto por mucho tiempo," Esteban roars as he attempts to throw a pair of fireballs only to watch them fizzle out. Suddenly the fire within his skin sizzles as he starts to stare down his hands. With each passing second, the flames weaken as with desperation he attempts one more. After spiraling from his hand, the flames fall inches from him before turning into broken embers. Disappearing, Esteban looks around before turning back to Col. Lins, seeing his smile.

"Incluso entonces sigues haciendo los mismos trucos que un perro viejo," Col. Lins replies as flames of his own appear through his body.

Before Esteban can make a move, Col. Lins looks down at his feet as they suddenly start to lift off the ground. As he gets higher, Esteban tumbles forward as he attempts to tackle him down. However as his hand wraps around Col. Lins's legs, the scorching rise of his body temperature burns Esteban. Releasing instantly, steam rises from Esteban's hands as he looks up to watch Col. Lins disappear into the dimly lit ceiling. Gone without a trace, Esteban continues to search when he turns back to Rafael who remains in the cage feet from him.

"¿Mis poderes se estan desvaneciendo, donde esta el?" Esteban asks as Rafael shrugs his shoulders before looking back at the roof.

"No lo veo, pero a quien le importa, salgamos de aquí," Rafael replies before turning his attention to the flimsy lock along the cage door.

Nodding his head, Esteban stumbles toward him as he goes to attempt to break him out when suddenly another round of static echoes across the room. Turning their attention around them, grinding chains break the monotony when the cage starts to shake. Struggling to hold on, Rafael braces himself as the cage makes its way upward as out of the static, laughter chimes inside the space. Getting just out of reach, Esteban attempts to fly upward only to make it inches from the floor before falling back down. Continuing to get higher, Rafael tries to reach his hand out to no avail as he gets farther away from Esteban.

"Si lo quieres entonces ven a buscarlo," Col. Lins voice chimes in when suddenly another set of lights turn on. Revealing a shadowy staircase along one of the walls, Esteban runs up as he starts to hold his side. Feeling the building pain of exhaustion, he makes his way to the bottom stair before placing his other hand along the railing. Skipping stairs along the way, he makes his way upward until he finally reaches the last one. Sitting steps from him, Esteban sees a massive doorway as Col. Lins stands at the opposite end. Facing out of the opening, Esteban makes his way inside carefully when suddenly the door closes behind him.

CHAPTER 18

Once inside, the lights around the room flicker about as it allows Esteban to see his new surroundings. Around him whether inside barrels or simply in piles along crates, things from his home stand throughout like piles of sugarcane and stacks of coconuts.

"Como sigue creciendo tu poder?" Esteban asks as his eyes reach a set of barrels.

"Mi poder permanece en mi piel en todo momento gracias a este calor caribeno," Col. Lins replies as he turns back to Esteban as he senses his inner deliberation.

"Como es possible que estamos en Estados Unidos?" Esteban asks as he feels his skin becoming drier by the second.

"Oh, por favor, heroe, estamos a millas de tu casa," Col. Lins replies as he extends his arms out.

"Entonces, como vas a conseguir café Cubano?" Esteban asks as he turns his focus back to the barrels beside him. Before Col. Lins can reply, Esteban desperately charges over to the barrels when a hand grabs him by the shoulder. Preventing him from getting further, Esteban attempts to look back when he sees Col. Lins glowing eyes before he punches Esteban in the ribs. Crumbling to the ground, Esteban tries to reach out for the barrels once more when Col. Lins grabs hold of his fingers. Unable to slide them free, Col. Lins snaps his fingers, sending pain jolting through every nerve of Esteban's body. Grimacing in pain as he wraps his other hand around the broken bones, his face reddens as tears slide down his cheeks.

"El café Cubano no es la unica bebida que puede desbloquear poderes," Col. Lins says as he stares into Esteban's trembling face. Continuing to stare, Col. Lins lifts a finger to the side of his face before sliding it down his cheek before pulling it forward. To Esteban's surprise, along the tip of the finger a brown liquid sits as it starts to slide down the sides. Then with a smirk, Col. Lins looks at it before pulling his hand back to his side. Before Esteban can move, Col. Lins shakes his head before turning around and taking a couple of steps away from him.

"Pagaras po resto," Esteban yells as he once more turns to the barrels at his side. Then as he attempts to take another dive toward it, Col. Lins hovers over and then kicks them through the stone wall. Creating a massive hole, the barrels tumble through the air as the opening reveals the hanging cage holding Rafael. As they slam to the ground, the liquid inside flows out onto the floor as it builds a puddle around the debris. Placing himself along the edge of the opening, he then turns to Rafael as tears continue to flow off his face.

Then before Rafael can speak another word, Esteban watches as his eyes widen causing him to look around. Just as his eyes can make it back, they watch as Col. Lins slams a spear of sugarcane into Esteban's sternum. Coming out of his back, Esteban struggles to maintain his footing as the warmth of blood starts to seep from his throat. As he feels it coming from out of the depths of the wound, Col. Lins pulls it out before delivering another haymaker to Esteban's face. Upon impact, the force sends Esteban into the air as Rafael looks on.

Weak and unstable, Esteban's eyes start to whiten as he falls through the air before landing with a splash into the puddle beneath him. As the liquid rains down, Col. Lins stands at the edge of the opening as Rafael starts to cry as he struggles to shake the chains of the cage. Rocking it back and forth, they both watch as Esteban's body lays lifeless along the ground as finally his eyes shut. Blood continuing to flow out, Col. Lins slams the bloody stalk onto the ground before disappearing from the opening. Leaving Rafael alone to watch his dad's broken body, his head sulks against the metal of the chains as he watches the tears fall from between the openings in the floor.

As the light of his life starts to dim, Esteban turns his head as he struggles to gasp for air. Feeling the oxygen as it barely enters his lungs, his eyes watch as a bright light appears in the room when suddenly a feminine figure appears as the darkness returns. Approaching him, the figure then kneels as it reveals a familiar face to Esteban as he struggles to keep his eyes open. Before him, his beloved Lorenza stands before him as she places her soft hand into his. Seeing her gentle smile, she tightens her grasp before picking him up. Feeling no pain as he stands back up, Esteban's eyes examine his body to see no wound when suddenly he looks behind him. At his heels remains his body as his eyes shut when he turns his attention to Lorenza who looks back at him.

"Has venido a llevarme al cielo?" Esteban asks as he watches Lorenza stand back up before delivering the gentlest of smiles.

"Si tu también me quisieras," Lorenza replies as suddenly the sounds between fall silent. As the wind passes through them, they then catch the sounds of Rafael's whimpering cries from above. Tampering Esteban's mood, he looks up at the cage before turning to Lorenza who shakes her head.

"Si no te hubieras ido, el no se habría visto envuelto el esto,"

Esteban replies as once more the sounds of his cries fade away.

"Esto es cierto, pero tienes la oportunidad de rescatarlo," Lorenza replies.

"Como puedo cuando no puedo derrotar a Col. Lins?" Esteban asks as he looks down at his broken body as it remains motionless on the ground.

"No ves lo que sucede a tu alrededor?" Lorenza replies as he motions her head toward the ground.

Turning his attention, Esteban watches as the level of the fluid lowers around his body. Continuing to look on, he spots remnants of sugarcane floating beside him as the wound along his sternum vanishes. Even the bones within his fingers repair themselves as he watches on from afar. Finally, the blood staining his skin and clothing fades away when Esteban turns toward Lorenza.

"Como es esto posible? No lo bebi," Esteban asks.

"Hay mas de una forma de introducir cosas en su sistema," Lorenza replies as she points toward the bare sternum of Esteban's body.

"Está bien, ¿pero incluso si tengo una segunda oportunidad, como puedo derrotario?" Esteban asks as Lorenza shakes her head.

"Intente usar otros elementos de Cuba además de su ardiente pasión por el hogar," Lorenza replies when suddenly things turn to darkness. Leaving them behind, suddenly the sounds of cracking thunder and gunshots ring out. As the smells of gunpowder and burnt sugarcane fill the space, Esteban looks around at his new location. He was somewhere he had been once before even as he stood in the center of rows of broken sugarcane stalks. Explosions ringing out in the distance, they start to hear footsteps as they look down to see a pair of figures approaching from the shadows. Watching on, his eyes open wide when he sees Diego step out from the shadows pushing a cart as a hand extends out. Then as they arrive at a hole where another man awaits them, the sound of crashing waves starts to overtake the gunshots in the distance.

"Por qué me has traído aquí para?" Esteban asks as he watches Diego stop the cart by the side of the hole in the ground. As the other man throws him a shovel, Lorenza and Esteban watch on as they prepare to take his body from the cart.

"Que te está dando Cuba aquí?" Lorenza asks as the motion around them freezes. Turning his attention around them, Esteban looks around from top to bottom before shifting his focus back to Lorenza. Watching as she makes her way to the nearby coastline, she kneels along the broken rocks along the sand as she places her hand into the waves as they remain frozen in time.

"Veo aqua de mar, Caña de azúcar y fuego de bombas explosivas," Esteban replies as the motion returns to the scene. Continuing the process, Esteban turns back to watch as the two men toss his body into the hole before freezing once more.

"Que otra cosa es lo que ves?" Lorenza asks as she points over to Diego as he stands at the side of the hole. Making his way over, Esteban stands at his side before looking at his friend's face. Over the dirt and gunpowder layers along his skin, tears start streaming down as they blend the layers upon contact. Even as the raindrops freeze all around, the tears separate themselves as some remain frozen still under his eyelids. That is when deep inside his spirit a feeling comes over Esteban, which causes him to look over at Lorenza.

"Amistad," Esteban replies as Lorenza smiles with his answer as the motions return. Watching on, they watch as Diego slams the shovel down along the edge before dropping to a knee beside the opening.

"Ahora usa estos elementos de Cuba para traer a casa a nuestro hijo," Lorenza replies as Esteban nods his head.

"Siempre supe que eras mi ángel guardian," Esteban replies as he watches Lorenza walk toward him. As the heels of his feet hang just shy of the edge of the opening, Lorenza grabs hold of his head and brings him forward. Delivering a kiss he shuts his eyes, and then reopens them to see her still standing there as a bolt of lightning cracks across the sky.

"Te amo Tormenta Cubano," Lorenza says as she pushes Esteban as he suddenly loses his balance.

As he falls below the layer of soil into the darkness below, his eyes shut as he feels his breath coming back into his lungs. Feeling the cold stone ground under his back, Esteban carefully opens his eyes to see the remnants of the brown liquid as it continues to evaporate. Before he could make a move, suddenly an apple that had fallen from the second-floor floats by his sight. Smirking as he takes it as a sign of his brother, he grabs it stealthily when the sounds of footsteps grow louder in the room. Splashing as they make their way closer, Esteban carefully closes his eyes when he feels a hand grab hold of his shirt before picking him up from the ground. As his body hangs in the air, the loose liquid rains down as he hears a snicker from the darkness beyond his eyelids.

"Lo dejo ir," Rafael's voice rings out.

"No te preocupes, pronto te uniras a el," Col. Lins replies, momentarily lessening his grip around Esteban's neck. That is when suddenly a fiery glow starts to grow underneath his tan skin as Esteban keeps his eyes shut.

Feeling the apple still just out of sight, Esteban senses Col. Lins shifting his attention. Then after a couple of seconds, Esteban jolts his eyes open as flames start to encapsulate his eyes. Startling him, Col. Lins releases his hold as he steps back just before Esteban smashes the apple along his face. Startling him as he stumbles through one of the tiny puddles left over, they watch as apple fragments crumble to the ground. Turning his attention back to Esteban a large red mark appears along Col. Lins cheek.

"Eso es para mi amigo loco de vuelta a casa," Esteban says before a delivering a round of punches to Col. Lins's face and sternum.

Screaming in anger, Col. Lins returns fire as he delivers a combination of his own before finishing it with a forearm to Esteban's temple. As both of their breaths quicken, Esteban drops to a knee as he turns his back to Col. Lins. Shaking his head, he looks around when suddenly the bloody spear slides into view as he grabs hold of it. Placing it along his arm so it remains hidden, Col. Lins charges forward before jumping into the air when suddenly Esteban turns back around. Swatting him out of the sky, Col. Lins slams into the stone wall, breaking loose pebbles as they land beside his body.

"Buen movimiento, pero sigues siendo un héroe de truco," Col. Lins mutters as he gets back to his feet. Revealing the damage done, Col. Lins's eyes dart to the side to see a slice of blood along the side of his face. Snickering, he then turns to Esteban to watch as the flames extinguish within his corneas. Chuckling, Col. Lins then takes a deep breath before unleashing a blend of wind and fire. Spiraling toward Esteban, Col. Lins watches in shock as Esteban squats before lifting into the sky. Avoiding the blast as he slams into the wall, Esteban hovers over the ground as he flies just feet above Rafael.

"Cuando tienes el corazon de Cuba tienes todo lo que necesitas," Esteban replies as he points the stalk of sugarcane toward Col. Lins. Roaring once more as the smoke from the blast fills the room, Col. Lins darts through as he pierces the layer to get toward Esteban.

Watching as Col. Lins breaks through the smoke, he then attempts to tackle Esteban who strikes him once more with the stalk as it starts to crack. Struggling to maintain his flight, Col. Lin's slides over to the top of Rafael's cage. Dragging his hand along the roof, he wraps his hand around one the chains as the force of his movement causes them to break. Leaving an opening, Rafael squats down as Col. Lins keeps his focus on Esteban when something behind him catches his eye.

Turning back, he drops down into the room before disappearing from beyond the opening. As Esteban cracks his knuckles in anticipation, he watches as Col. Lins reappears with large military trunk before slamming it down just beside the edge of the opening. Bending down, Col. Lins opens it up before pulling out a massive bottle from its confines. Turning his attention to Esteban, he then pops the cork out before flames begin to reach into the depths of his eyes.

"Solo te vas a debilitar," Esteban says as he floats back toward the far side of the room.

"Oh, mira la poderosa Tormenta Cubano esta tratando de ayudarme," Col. Lins chuckles as the flames within his body start to channel upwards. Leaning back his head, smoke starts to swirl from his nostrils when suddenly he comes forward as he unleashes a massive fireball with the aid of the bottle before him. Dropping Rafael to the cage floor with his hands over his head, the flames spread throughout the room until it starts to approach Esteban. Getting closer as the glow starts to reflect within his eyes, Esteban looks down at his hands before turning his focus back to the approaching attack.

"Te lo adverti," Esteban replies as he places his hands out when suddenly the sounds of thunder start to reverberate through the room. Before the flames can do any harm, suddenly a burst of wind rises from the ground toward the ceiling. Crashing into the rock formations above, stones start to fall as they miss all three of the men below. Once the last piece of debris has fallen and the smoke clears, Esteban looks on as Col. Lins throws the bottle in his direction. Watching as liquid spews out of the top of the bottle, he watches as it falls before it gets any closer to him. Intensifying his anger, Col. Lins digs down into the locker before him and pulls out a set of axes before swinging them recklessly around him. Then as they arrive at his side, he takes a large step forward before attempting to fly off to attack Esteban.

However, as he is preparing to do so, Rafael reaches him and snags him by the foot and trips Col. Lins.

Snarling as he looks down causing him to tremble, Col. Lins turns his focus back to Esteban as once more he attempts to fly up into the air. This time his feet lift off when instantly they return as once more he attempts to lift off. However, after failing a second time, he then looks around in confusion as he looks all around his arms before looking back at Esteban.

"Que has hecho?" Col. Lins screams as he tries another couple of times to fly to no avail.

"Yo nada era todo tu," Esteban replies as he smirks at his struggles and fails. However, watching on, Esteban swiftly disappears when Col. Lins turns his attention to Rafael standing below his feet.

As Col. Lins takes aim with the axes alongside him, he attempts an attack when suddenly Esteban dives downward. Before it can get halfway, Esteban slams into him as both men tumble and roll into the various objects around the room.

First to his feet, Esteban rises and jumps all over Col. Lins, delivering kick after punch after kick. Then as he attempts another blow, Col. Lins attempts to reach for an axe that lay by his side. Before his fingertips can touch the handle, Esteban steps down onto his wrist as it causes his fingers to flail about the ground.

With his hand stuck, Esteban wails a couple of more shots into Col.

Lins's prone ribs before delivering a forearm to the side of his face. His hand coming to a rest along the ground, Esteban releases his hold when he steps off before turning his attention to Rafael. Smirking with every step, suddenly he turns around and grabs hold of the pointy end of a spear that Col. Lins is wielding. Twisting it from his grasp, Col. Lins retreats with his hands up as Esteban turns back to see Rafael awaiting him.

"No eres mas' que un hombre roto," Esteban says as he turns his back to Col. Lins. Angering him further, Col. Lins charges at him once more when Esteban side steps before he can wrap his arms around him. Just before he can fall to the ground, Esteban grabs him by the shreds of a shirt and slams him into a pile of coconuts nearby. Groaning in pain, Col. Lins watches Esteban turn his attention back to the cage door. Placing his hands on top of the handle, he then snaps it off before tossing it to the ground. As it ricochets into the wall, the door opens as Rafael jumps into Esteban's embrace. Once free of the shadows within the cage, the two men make their way toward the doorway along the back of the room.

"Vamos a casa hijo mio," Esteban says as he places his arm around Rafael's shoulders.

"Te refieres a las casa que vole," Col. Lins replies as the two men stop to see him standing in front of the opening. Then before they can say another word, he slams his hand around a large lever along the wall. With a single flip, suddenly the room starts to shake violently as the doorway behind them starts to crumble apart. Trapping them from going in that direction, the two men watch as large sections of rock and stone fall behind Col. Lins before disappearing.

As Esteban removes his arm from around his son, Col. Lins shakes his head before wagging his finger. Once the vibration stops, he then reaches into the locker once more as he pulls out a military soldier's belt with grenades lining the length of it.

"No ves que estas perdido?" Esteban asks as he looks over at his son.

"Yo no lo veo asi," Col. Lins replies as he starts to wave the grenades back and forth.

"Es que todo lo que tienes son algunas granadas Viejas?" Esteban asks.

"Debajo de mi hay cientos de lanzas hechas de Caña de azúcar robadas de tu patria," Col. Lins says as he looks down behind him.

"Así que lo que?" Esteban asks.

"De cualquier manera vas a morir," Col. Lins replies as he begins to pull the pin out of the grenade toward the bottom. As he reaches for it, Esteban leans over and grabs hold of the axe by his foot and throws it towards him. Just before Col. Lins can pull it from the mechanism, the blade slices his hand clean off. Blood flowing from the wound, Col. Lins eyes widen as the axe falls to the ground along with his hand. Once gone, he then turns to Esteban to find him no longer there. As Rafael stands alone, Col. Lins turns around to see Esteban waiting for him to shift his focus.

"Esto es para Cuba," Esteban yells as he grabs Col. Lins before tossing him over the edge. As he starts to fall, Rafael runs up as the two men watch Col. Lins slam into the spears as the life from his body starts to fade. Beside him the belt of grenades bounces inches from his fingertips as Esteban turns to Rafael.

"Como vamos a salir?" Rafael asks as Esteban turns his attention toward the night sky. Seeing the moon lighting the opening above, Esteban smirks as once more he places his arm around Rafael's shoulders.

"Agarrate fuerte hijo," Esteban replies as Rafael gives him a hug just in time for his feet to lift off the ground. Once the two were in the air, they start to head out through the opening as beneath them Col. Lins screams in pain. Getting further away as the scream muffles to a whisper, Rafael looks over at Esteban as the two men fly over the ocean. Getting further away, suddenly they spot a helicopter familiar to Esteban. With a smile, the two men fly closer as they spot the saluting pilot inside the cockpit. Dodging a couple of clouds along the way, they land inside safely as Rafael takes a seat in the center. Turning his attention back to the drifting landmass, Esteban looks on when suddenly an explosion erupts from the opening.

Flames shooting upwards as smoke spreads through the night, the pilot swings the helicopter to avoid the shockwaves. Feeling minimal turbulence, they put themselves back on course when Rafael looks back over to Esteban as he sits down beside him.

"Como supiste que lo lograría?" Esteban asks as he puts on his seatbelt.

"Tu eres el Tormenta Cubano," the pilot replies as he nods his head before turning his attention to Rafael who sits quietly.

"A dónde vamos?" Rafael asks as the pilot turns back to see Esteban as he looks at both men.

"De vuelta a casa y lejos de este lugar," Esteban replies as the pilot nods his head before turning his attention back to the wheel.

"Que nos espera alli?" Rafael asks as the helicopter begins to move forward.

"No lo sé hijo mio, pero sé que una manzana loca espera tu regreso," Esteban replies as Rafael nods his head. Then as the father and son sit back in their seats, the helicopter takes off through the night sky just above the peaceful sea.

Reviews are crucial to indie authors like me. If you enjoyed this book, please leave me a review! It helps me and it helps others find my book, too! Thank you!

Also, check out my other books:

The Adventures of George and Reggie

The Adventures of George and Reggie 2:
King Orcan's Revenge

Murdio

BloodMinazue

Pakul

The Ringmaster of My Creative Imagination